AN OXFORD REVENGE

An utterly gripping page-turner

FAITH MARTIN
writing as

MAXINE BARRY

JOFFE
BOOKS

First published by Joffe Books, London 2020
www.joffebooks.com

First published in Great Britain 1999
as *Moth to the Flame*

**Please join our mailing list for free Kindle books
and new releases.**

ISBN 978-1-78931-358-1

ONE

Paddington Station on a cold and draughty February morning was not, Davina Granger thought wryly, her favourite place in the whole wide world. As she made her way to the platform she wanted, she could feel many interested male eyes boring into her.

At thirty, she knew that her slender and fit body still moved very well, though not provocatively. She'd never sashayed to attract a man in her life and wasn't about to start now. Her short spiky blonde hair drew all eyes to her delicate, elfin-shaped face, and she was well aware that men found her full lips fascinating. Her huge green eyes even more so.

She pulled her heavy woollen coat tighter around her, shivering slightly, and tried not to remember that she'd been in Bali just a fortnight ago. She tried even harder not to dwell on where she was going now, and why.

The upper body muscles on her five-foot seven-inch figure contracted fluidly as she hefted her heavy case up some stairs. She usually worked out with weights every morning, enjoyed swimming regularly and jogged whenever the weather permitted. She knew she'd never been fitter. She'd also just recently finished a year of self-defence classes with the judo-master husband of her best friend.

1

She walked to the electronic board, found the departure time for the train she wanted, and headed towards the ticket office.

Something in the back of her mind told her it would be much better to turn around and go home. Much safer. Much easier. But Davina Granger wasn't always sensible. She knew that and lived with it. She knew all about truth and consequences. Oh yes. She knew all about that.

She stood dutifully in line for the ticket counter, thinking about Bali and all the other places she'd been as she wandered the world in search of inspiration. Any student of human nature would have picked her out of the crowd immediately. It was not her unusual looks or her air of aloofness that made her so different from all the rest, but a sad kind of aloneness that seemed to encompass her.

As she approached the arched window, the ticket seller looked up, his tired brown eyes widening slightly. The woman was stunning. Such big green eyes. Such a striking face. He didn't usually like these close-cut spiky hairdos on women. He preferred his females with long hair that a man could run his fingers through. But, somehow, this woman was different.

'A ticket to Oxford, please.' Although the voice didn't snap, wasn't impatient or demanding, he found himself suddenly jumping to attention. Blushing. Feeling oddly guilty for staring at her. He lowered his eyes, fiddling with the machine at his elbow.

'A return ticket?'

Davina felt her lips twist into a grim smile. Her large green eyes seemed to glow, just for a second. The ticket seller found his breath catching in his throat. For one instant there, he'd thought that she looked almost feral. Then Davina's smile seemed to flicker out, like a candle being snuffed in a breeze.

'No,' she said, her voice a dull tone. 'Just one way.'

For some reason, the ticket seller shivered. There was something ominous in the way she'd said that.

As Davina took the ticket, it felt oddly cold in her hand. She glanced down, a little surprised to see that her hand was shaking. She tried to stop the fine trembling from invading her body, but it was hard. For this really was strictly a one-way trip — in more ways than one.

She took a seat and waited for her train to be designated a platform number, taking calming breaths. She wanted nothing to distract her for the next few months. She had to get herself under control.

She supposed it would have been easier to take her car, a well-preserved bottle-green E-type Jaguar. But she'd decided that, since she was going to Oxford, she might as well go the whole hog. She'd buy a bicycle when she got there, and cycle around the city instead. It was important that she fitted in. She had to project the right image.

Davina knew quite a lot about projecting images. In some form or another, she'd been doing it all her life.

When her train came, she found an empty seat and settled herself down, ignoring the man opposite, who kept flickering looks at her from behind the papers he was reading.

Davina watched the graffiti-bedaubed walls and depressing grey cityscape rush by with eyes that took it all in and processed it, almost automatically, into words. Words were her lifeblood. Words were her best friend. And, sometimes, her worst enemy. Words, she was sometimes convinced, were the only thing she was good at.

Twenty minutes later, grazing horses and swan- and coot-filled rivers took over. For all her travels, there was still no place like England. No place like home.

Home. Davina's lips twisted in a sudden, surprised grimace of pain. No. She would not think of home.

Once it had been a warm place, a hectic, unfashionably decorated house in Hastings. Home had meant her mother and David. Her mother, who'd always encouraged her in her ambition, and David, her much younger stepbrother, full of cheek, charm and mischief. Now home was no longer hectic. No longer warm. It was just a house where her mother grieved, and David's ghost haunted every room.

She still felt guilty at leaving her mother behind, all alone. But she'd had no other choice. If Davina had told her what she was planning, her mother would only have tried to talk her out of it.

Davina saw the green fields blur into a velvet mist, and realised she was on the verge of crying. Again. Grimly she blinked. Focused. Breathed deeply. She itched to snatch up some paper and write a scathing, hot and bitter poem about repressed grief. But she didn't, of course, and the world slowly righted itself.

Then, nearly an hour to the minute after leaving London, the train pulled into Oxford Station.

She was wearing a long lilac skirt and a cream camisole which hugged her gently swelling breasts, topped with a gauzy cardigan in a darker shade of lilac. She was slender-waisted, but had a powerful elegance, and as she lowered her case from the overhead rack, it caught her fellow passenger's attention.

She glanced at the man staring at her, but the expression in her large green eyes was not what he was expecting. It was neither the pleased look of a woman who dressed to be admired, nor the scornful look of a man-hater. The woman looked at him . . . well, with a kind of blank indifference.

Davina slipped into her long, warm woollen coat, and left the train.

A nineteen-year-old student, who was just getting on the train as she was stepping off, suddenly did a comical double-take. The student, a woman with long black hair and china-blue eyes, hesitated visibly, one foot on the train, one foot on the platform. She was in her first year of a three-year BA course in English Literature, and Davina's challenging, clear-eyed, defiant face was familiar to anyone who read modern poetry.

For a moment, Alicia Norman wanted to forget about the train and her weekend trip home. Instead, she wanted to rush after the greatest living poet in the country (in her opinion) and . . . what? Alicia laughed at herself. Ask for her autograph, like some star-struck fan? She shook her head and stepped onto the train, telling herself to act her age.

But as she took a seat, she craned her head to watch the striking blonde woman walk up the platform with a ground-covering ease that Alicia really envied. Like a fox, the woman looked as though she could lope along for miles without even thinking about it. Alicia herself was too short to be able to glide that smoothly.

Unaware of her silent fan club, Davina stood at the top of a short flight of steps and looked around. The city heaved with traffic, and seemed, from this angle, like any other modern city anywhere in the world. So much for dreaming spires, punts on the Isis, mellow stone colleges and scatty, absent-minded academics in black gowns and mortar boards, she thought with a self-mocking laugh.

She had never gone to university, had never wanted to. At sixteen she couldn't wait to leave school, being too eager to taste real life and all it had to offer. Besides, why study what other people had written when all she cared about was what she could write herself? Davina smiled at the naive, shallow, greedy little teenager she had once been. Well, she'd seen life all right. And learned all that it had to teach her.

She walked to the taxi rank and shouted over the noisy rattle of the engine, 'St Bede's please.' The taxi driver lifted a hand to indicate he'd heard her and pulled away. Davina looked around her with little interest. She was too nervous, thinking about what lay ahead of her, to pay much attention to her surroundings. What if it all went wrong? What if she couldn't think of a way of seeing justice done? She shook her head. One thing at a time. She was tough, clever and resourceful. She would find a way.

She forced herself to relax, to study the famous city unfolding all around her. After all, she was going to have to live here for the next four months.

The cab pulled up at traffic lights, where the Randolph Hotel stood to her right, facing the Ashmolean Museum on her left.

Davina's eyes glimmered as she looked at the Gothic columns of the museum. Now that was more what she expected of Oxford. Class. Elegance. Old-World style. Across the road was the Martyrs' Memorial, with its flock of appreciative pigeons, and beyond that, the pale facade of Balliol. And, suddenly, she felt the city begin to charm her.

Without warning, as the Carfax clock chimed midday, Davina realised that she wasn't in a city that could be just any other city in the world. She was in a city that could only be Oxford.

The taxi indicated left and turned up St Giles. In the autumn, she knew, it played host to a famous centuries-old fair. She recognised the modest building that was St Cross, one of the smaller of Oxford's thirty-plus individual colleges. They passed Browns, the famous restaurant, and on up the Woodstock Road. Trees grew everywhere. Nestled among shops and offices were glimpses of cloisters, crenellated walls, ancient mullioned windows. The very air seemed to breathe a sense of history. Her sensitive, writer's soul felt a frisson of kinship. Here, famous figures throughout history had lived, studied, loved, died.

The cab slowed to a crawl. And there, sandwiched between Somerville College and the old Radcliffe Infirmary, was the ancient oak gateway to St Bede's itself.

Davina got out and tipped the driver heavily. For a few long moments she stood on the pavement, looking at the huge double gates, and the smaller gate set within it that was open, admitting a steady stream of visitors.

So, this was it.

After weeks of wangling, planning, worming her way in, she had finally arrived. The lair of the enemy.

Davina picked up her case and stepped carefully inside, her chin held high, her lips set in a grim determined line. Immediately to her left was a huge arched stained-glass window, and a building that was so ecclesiastical it could only be the college chapel. To her right was a much smaller, modern building, the porter's lodge. She stepped inside, smiled, and asked if she could leave her suitcase there for an hour. She was cheerfully informed that she could. She left hastily, aware that the receptionist had recognised her name and had been on the verge of offering a gushing speech of welcome.

Davina knew, of course, that she would receive the red-carpet treatment the moment her presence was public knowledge, but she was not quite ready for that yet. She wanted to explore. Get her bearings. Gird her loins.

She walked into the first of the quads and reached into her shoulder bag for the copy of the college prospectus she'd sent away for. This glossy brochure, complete with artistic photographs and blurb, informed her that she was currently standing in St Agatha Quad.

She tried to recall who St Agatha was, and for what she'd been canonised, but without much success. She made a mental note to read up on her. Those ancient martyrs were usually fascinating people. Perhaps a poem about a modern-day version? Davina laughed at herself. Whatever else she was, no matter what was going on in her life at a given moment, she was always a poet. On the lookout for inspiration everywhere she went. Taking mental notes. She was sure that on her deathbed she'd be composing a mourning poem for herself in her head.

Telling herself firmly to stick to the matters in hand, she once more consulted the brochure. St Bede's, she read, was named after the Venerable Bede, who'd been born around AD 673. He'd been a theological historian of wide acclaim, which accounted for the very large Theology and History departments at St Bede's. Fortunately for her, the college also boasted one of the largest English Literature intakes of any Oxford college, as well as a famous library.

Davina glanced around her at mellow Cotswold stone residences, gardens frothing with colour even in this inhospitable month, and a large stone cross. A quick glance at her prospectus told her that the residence in front of her, its facade smothered with winter-flowering yellow jasmine, was a student residence called Webster. Named, so she was informed, after John Webster, the Elizabethan dramatist who'd written, among other things, *The Duchess of Malfi*. Of course, Davina already knew that. She'd read the play some years ago — when she'd grown up enough to realise that reading the greats and classics was hardly a betrayal of her principles. Indeed, it might actually do her some good.

She walked slowly, reluctantly, forward and stood in front of the large stone cross. It was, of course, a war memorial. And on it, listed in sad, carved lines, were the names of St Bede's fallen, young men who'd studied here in the halcyon days before the wars, and then lost their lives on battlefields in Flanders and Germany. Davina's lips twisted as a great rush of bitterness and pity washed over her. Such a waste.

So much futility. If women ruled the world, such insanities would never happen . . . She moved quickly on, past a rather unattractive car park and towards a much more interesting and attractive feature — the college clock, set squarely in the middle of yet another quad — Wallace Quad this time — with four massive white dials facing north, south, east and west.

She checked her watch, saw that the clock was right on time and gave it a friendly pat of congratulation as she walked on past it.

Opposite her was an ancient stretch of drystone walling and a very attractive arch, showing glimpses of green velvet lawns, ponds and more stone facades beyond it. Becket Arch, the very helpful prospectus informed her. And through it, the main college gardens, croquet lawn, and the other student residences of Wolsey and Walton. Once again, she recognised the names. Wolsey, named after the cardinal who was Henry VIII's ill-fated advisor. And Walton, named after Izaak, author of *The Compleat Angler*, written in the seventeenth century.

But as she stepped through Becket Arch, Davina Granger was not thinking about that esteemed fellow wordsmith and fisherman. She was thinking only that, within those many rooms, he was working. Perhaps giving a tutorial to one of his students. Or perhaps working on his own latest creation.

Dr Gareth Lacey. The much-published Dr Gareth Lacey, one of St Bede's three much-respected, lauded and venerated English dons. Specialities: modern poetry and the Romantics.

She forced her hands, which had clenched into fists by her sides, to relax, but she could still feel the imprint from her fingernails where they had cut into her palms. Davina really must learn to control the rush of rage and hatred that washed over her whenever she so much as even thought of his name. She must force herself to keep a distance. Step back, think coldly, logically. Otherwise she would destroy herself.

And not Gareth Lacey.

She turned and made her way to the main entrance to St Bede's famous library. She very much needed peace and quiet, a place to sit and think and recover.

The library was one of the oldest buildings in the college, and as she walked along the cold stone floors, worn down by a procession of Oxford students who'd studied in these hallowed, narrow rooms since before the reign of Queen Elizabeth I, she found herself trembling again. A fine shivering in her lithe, conditioned muscles. A weakness that had nothing to do with the physical, but everything to do with mental stress.

Davina was apt to be over-emotional. She knew that. Her teachers had told her mother so when she was nine and had reacted so badly to the death of her stepfather. As a poet, having a fine, sensitive nature was a huge asset. But it left her extremely vulnerable to the barbs of everyday living.

She pushed open a heavy door and found herself looking down a long tunnel lined with books. Nothing but books as far as the eye could see. In bays, stretched out along the length of the building, were heavy wooden tables and comfortable red velvet-backed chairs. Some were empty, others held students who glanced up from their reading and gazed at her with vague curiosity. Davina breathed deeply of the musty, dusty, wonderful atmosphere that only books could produce. The floorboards underneath were soft and spongy, as was the ancient, faded red carpet. She felt the building welcome her like an old friend.

She moved along the line of books — heading unerringly for the English Literature section. There, she found everything from Thackeray to Dylan Thomas, John Donne to Ted Hughes, Shakespeare's complete works to Virginia Woolf. She slowly sat down at an empty table and took a long, slow, deep breath.

Steady.

She was here now. She'd made it. Step one in her plans was accomplished and completed.

Nothing was going to stop her now.

The destruction of Gareth Lacey could begin.

TWO

The principal of St Bede's, Lord St John James, known simply as Sin-Jun to his friends, walked briskly towards the lodge. He was a well-preserved man in his early sixties and was looking forward to meeting their latest VIP. After arranging honorary fellowship status for Davina Granger for Hilary Term, he was the current darling of the English department.

When he stepped through the door into the small, office-like interior, however, he stopped abruptly. He'd expected the most famous and controversial modern female poet of her generation to look . . . well, different. Like a female bulldog perhaps. Ready to chew him up and spit him out.

'Hello. You must be Lord St John James?' The voice wasn't what he'd been expecting either. Soft. Feminine. At total odds with the short, spiky, defiant haircut and level, challenging, but quite delightful green eyes.

'Er . . . yes. Please, call me Sin-Jun. It's a lot less work for the tongue.'

'Thank you so much for inviting me here this term,' she said sweetly. 'I can't tell you how much I'm looking forward to being a part of a college like St Bede's.'

Sin-Jun beamed, utterly charmed. 'The pleasure, and the privilege, my dear, I assure you, are all ours. Well now,

I'm sure you'd like to see your rooms and . . . er . . . freshen up, yes?' he asked tentatively. The trouble with so-called liberated women was that you never knew when you were going to get your head chewed off for saying something sexist. And since Sin-Jun hadn't the least idea what constituted a sexist remark, he was naturally wary.

Davina picked up her suitcase and smiled. 'Thank you. That would be nice.'

He began filling her in about some of Oxford's traditions as they walked out into St Agatha Quad, and, much to her relief, past Webster. It meant she was in either Wolsey or Walton — just where she wanted to be.

She was glad the principal so obviously approved of her — it was vital that she get as many members of the college's hierarchy eating out of her hand as possible. She was going to have to entrench herself quickly and deeply in college life if she was to learn all the secrets and weaknesses of one Dr Gareth Lacey.

'This is Wolsey,' Sin-Jun said. 'We've got a very nice set of rooms free here.' As he talked, he opened a large door that led into a dark but charming hallway with a carved wooden staircase and big crystal chandelier.

'You can almost smell the centuries in here,' Davina murmured, instantly aware of the feeling of antiquity that assailed her. 'I'm going to love it, I can tell.'

And Walton was right across the gardens. Easy access to her enemy, but with just enough distance to provide her with breathing space when she needed it. 'It's perfect.'

'Your rooms are on the first floor — a corner suite. It'll be quite quiet because you don't have noisy student neighbours on every side of you.'

The rooms he led her to were some of the most elegant and interesting Davina had ever seen.

The door opened on to the study, where a log fire already burned in the grate. Davina instantly walked towards it. 'It's lovely. But I'm not sure I'd know how to keep it going?' she said, watching the flames as they hypnotically danced their way up the chimney.

'Oh, the scouts will do that for you,' Sin-Jun said quickly.

Davina surmised that in Oxford scouts were the members of staff responsible for cleaning the rooms, serving the fellows, and generally keeping the place running. She smiled. 'I can see I'm going to be spoiled rotten.'

She glanced round at the worn but comfortable sofa and large leather armchair. She walked towards the window, where the surface of an ancient desk caught the fading winter light. There were some undistinguished but genuine daubs from the seventeenth and eighteenth centuries hanging on the walls, and faded but lovely green velvet curtains framed a view across the croquet lawns.

'It's wonderful — just what I need to inspire me in my work. I dare say I'll spend a lot of my time in the libraries though. And,' she added, oh-so-casually, 'consulting various English Literature fellows. St Bede's has three, I understand? Of course, the man I need to see most is the fellow who specialises in modern poetry?'

Sin-Jun's face lit up. 'Ah! Yes, that'll be Gareth. Dr Gareth Lacey? You may have read his books?'

Davina smiled. Like a tiger. 'Oh yes. I've read every word Dr Lacey has ever written.' She didn't add that her interest in his books had only been recent. Very recent.

Sin-Jun beamed. 'He's eager to meet you too, I assure you.'

Davina smiled. 'That's nice,' she said, her green eyes glowing like newly cut and polished emeralds.

'Well, I'll leave you to unpack,' Sin-Jun rubbed his hands briskly. 'Oh, we're having pre-dinner cocktails in the SCR — the Senior Common Room — at five o'clock. I've invited several English fellows from other colleges to join us, and of course our own scholars and exhibitioners. I'm sure they'll give you a generous welcome,' he added, before taking his leave.

Inside her small domain, Davina made a brief tour. There was a large bedroom with a huge four-poster bed but rather inadequate wardrobe space, and a small kitchenette off the study. An antiquated bathroom completed the suite.

She nodded in satisfaction. She couldn't have asked for things to go better. Now, all she had to do was prepare for drinks and dinner, and her first meeting with the enemy.

She glanced at her watch. Nearly four. She hurried to the bathroom, and while the vast claw-footed tub was filling, quickly and methodically unpacked. She added gardenia bath oil, returned to her bedroom, stripped, and picked up her two hand weights. She'd learned to use them when she went to America, just after her seventeenth birthday, and had shared a flat near Muscle Beach.

Since then she'd published six books of poetry, won every major prize going, and travelled all over the world, working in all kinds of weird and wonderful places, doing all kinds of weird and wonderful jobs to keep her head above financial water.

She trained only in order to be fit and gave her actual physical attractiveness very little thought at all. She wore her hair so short because it meant she didn't have to bother with it. The fact that men seemed to either love it or loathe it that way worried her not one whit.

Never in her life had Davina actively sought to attract a man. Until now.

She stopped pumping the weights and climbed into the bath. As she soaked, she thought about her campaign. She simply had to get close to Gareth Lacey. Had to ferret out his every weakness, his every dream, the way he thought, the way he lived, what made him tick. And the easiest way she knew to do that was to get him interested in her.

She hoped he wasn't married. She closed her eyes briefly, appalled at the thought. She didn't want any woman to suffer because of what she was doing. No. If he was married, she'd have to find another way. But she'd make it one of the first things she tried to find out at the cocktail party.

She opened her eyes again and took a deep steadying breath. OK. She was not going to compromise her principles, not even for Lacey. Especially not for Lacey.

She sat up abruptly and reached for the shampoo. But as she did so, Davina began to cry. She wasn't aware of it at first. Then a small drip hit the back of her hand and she raised it to her cheek, giving a small grimace as her hand came away wet with salty tears.

Angrily she brushed the tears away.

She'd cried for David when she read her mother's letter, telling her that he was dead. (She'd been in Australia at the time, working on a sheep farm.) She'd cried for him on the plane over. She'd cried for him at his funeral. She'd cried for him as she reread his letters about how unhappy he was at St Bede's. Cried as she read how Dr Gareth Lacey was driving him to despair. Cried all those dark, lonely, bewildered nights after his funeral.

It was time to stop crying now.

She got out of the tub and rubbed herself vigorously, leaving her body glowing healthily all over. Next she rubbed her head with a hand towel, which was all her short hair needed to dry it, then walked into the bedroom. She slipped on a pair of plain white panties and walked to the wardrobe. There she reached in and drew out her favourite dress. It was pale lilac, shot through with silver thread, and had delicate spaghetti straps that left her shoulders and back bare. Since she'd not long returned from Bali, she still retained the last golden gleam of a light tan. Against such skin, the pale lilac and silver contrasted sharply. The dress had a definite 1920s style, with a fringe at the hem that swayed with every movement of her body. The simple neckline cunningly hugged her braless breasts, but the material was thick with silver thread only very subtly hinting at the nipples beneath. She reached for a comb and ran it though her hair, which was silky clean from the shampooing, smelled of gardenias, and gleamed a rich gold.

Her face needed very little make-up, but she added a touch of blusher, just to accentuate her cheekbones and jawline. A hint of silver over her green eyes transformed them into silver-lined emeralds, and a touch of plum-coloured lip-gloss to her full lips provided a feast for male eyes. No man would know what to look at first.

She smiled. Good. All she had to do now was wait.

* * *

Sin-Jun met her in front of the green baize door of the SCR dead on time. As she slipped out of her coat, Davina heard him gulp. When he pushed open the door, the noise level hit her like a physical blow. She never had liked walking into a crowded room, even though, by now, she should be used to it. Most people seemed to think of her as a party animal.

Slowly, bit by bit, the noise level dropped into dead silence. Sin-Jun beamed as the faces turned their way. 'Ah, here we are . . . er . . . Miss Granger.'

Davina glanced around the assembly. From her level-eyed gaze, not one of the people there would ever guess at the agonies of shyness she'd had to overcome in her teenage years.

'This is Dr Fletcher, our senior English Literature fellow.' Sin-Jun introduced her to the first of many, and suddenly the worst was over. The noise began to hum politely again. Davina smiled at a tall, ginger-haired man, who shook her hand and raised an eyebrow at the firmness of her grip. 'I've read all your work of course, but I'm a metaphysical poetry man myself,' he smiled at her, instantly putting her on to more solid ground. She could talk poetry with anybody — even the best that Oxford had to offer.

Davina smiled. 'Ask not for whom the bell tolls . . .' she murmured the famous quote from John Donne, which had been hijacked by Ernest Hemingway, with such notable success.

And so it began. Davina began to talk to Dr Fletcher about John Donne's famous conversion to Catholicism. Others eavesdropped openly. People circulated. Drank. Nibbled canapés.

During that first conversation, she learned that the other English Lit fellow was currently away sick, and also that Dr Lacey was an avid fan of hers. From there, she learned that Dr Lacey was a widower of some years' standing, and that he'd rowed for the Oxford Boat Race team back in his student days. He'd been educated right there at St Bede's, apparently, and had no current amour. 'He's right over there, talking to Rex Jimson-Clarke, a Theology fellow,' her helpful companion finished obligingly. Following the direction of Dr Fletcher's pointing finger, Davina saw two men holding the ubiquitous sherry glasses, talking under a massive reproduction of the St Bede's coat of arms.

One of them was tall, easily over six feet, with dark wings of hair that swept down across a high intelligent forehead. He looked to be in his mid-thirties. There was something about the way he stood, an air of allure about him, that had Davina's skin itching. It was nearly a year since she'd broken up with Jax, her last boyfriend, and she'd been celibate ever since. Now, something about the dark, handsome stranger had her body reminding itself of the fact.

Resolutely she turned her attention to the man next to him. He was a good decade older, portly, beaming-of-face. A bit like a teddy bear. Davina's lips twisted as she contemplated the enemy, then she quickly untwisted them. She simply couldn't afford to give away her true feelings this early on in the game. She turned to smile up at Dr Fletcher. 'I know it's early days yet, but I'd really like a word with Dr Lacey. As the resident modern-poetry expert, I was hoping . . .'

But before she could achieve her goal, Sin-Jun chose that moment to tap his glass with a spoon. Amazing that that tiny ringing sound could stop the conversation of a roomful of people in mid-flow.

'Ladies and gentlemen. As you know, we're gathered together tonight to welcome our latest honorary fellow to St Bede's.' Everyone glanced her way, from the third-year scholar in English, who was dying to ask Davina about a rather obscure line in one of her lesser-known poems, to the emeritus professor in Oriental Studies, who was soon to see his ninetieth birthday.

'Davina Granger, one of our most celebrated modern poets, has been commissioned to edit an anthology of modern poetry. St Bede's has been lucky enough to attract Miss Granger into our hallowed halls for the duration of Hilary Term, while she writes her foreword for this project, and selects her choices. I'm sure our excellent English section in the library will be seeing much of her.'

There was a ripple of genuinely excited applause. Especially from the librarian, who was positively salivating.

'I have no doubt her choices will be cosmopolitan, insightful and, I daresay, controversial.' There was another ripple of even more excited applause.

Davina smiled vaguely and wondered, cynically, how many of them were actually interested in the project, and how many of them just wanted to know if what the newspapers said about her affair with Jax Coulson was true.

Jax Coulson was Hollywood's current favourite, and he'd recently given a statement that his four-year-long relationship with the English poetess Davina Granger had come to an end because she'd been too wild for him.

'Ladies and gentlemen, I'd like to propose a toast — to Davina Granger. Who, as I'm sure you know, has recently been shortlisted for the Nobel Prize for Literature.'

There was a huge barrage of applause.

Davina had heard she'd been shortlisted for the most prestigious prize of all, but it was on the day after David's funeral, and she had hardly taken it in. She'd had other things to think about. Like, why her brother had committed suicide . . . ?

Besides, she didn't rate her chances of actually winning the prize as very high. She was still young. Still female. Still too controversial to be seriously considered. But, in an environment like this, she realised that it was regarded as a very real honour indeed. She'd have to remember to play it for all it was worth and use it to impress Dr Gareth Lacey. She was willing to use any and every weapon at her disposal in order to destroy the man who'd destroyed David.

As the applause died down, and a second-year exhibitioner in English plucked up the courage to sidle up to her with a copy of her third book of poetry and a pen, she watched the portly figure of Dr Gareth Lacey as he talked to the tall, extremely good-looking academic beside him. She signed the book, talked to the student about her desire to start a really meaningful literary magazine, and casually wandered over to her target. Long before she got to them, of course, both men stopped talking and turned to look at her. The staid surroundings of the SCR highlighted her unique and exotic beauty, and both men were openly dazzled.

It was the tall, handsome man beside Dr Lacey who first caught her attention. As she got closer, she could see that he had large, stormy-grey eyes, thick-lashed, set in one of the most handsome faces she'd ever seen. That square chin and firm jaw were really rather sexy indeed. She swallowed back a sudden pang of desire. Now was not the time for that. But the next instant she noticed that he had such long, sensitive hands, and had a sudden image of those hands on her body. Touching her. Caressing her. She blinked, surprised by the swiftness and intensity of the feeling. Her body actually tingled, where she imagined his fingers . . .

Angrily she dragged her eyes from him. It was the other man she needed to concentrate on. The enemy. Fortunately for her, there was nothing the least sexually attractive about him. Round, red-faced, he looked like somebody's idea of a human version of Winnie-the-Pooh.

Funny how outward appearances could be so deceptive.

She remembered David's last despairing letter to her, describing this man as a monster in human form. A jealous, manipulative, sarcastic, spiteful presence in his life.

She'd been disturbed by the sheer force of her usually placid brother's prose. She'd written back, advising him to ask to be assigned to another tutor.

Such realistic, prosaic advice. Such useless, inadequate, uncaring advice. If only she'd known how desperate David was. How desperate this man had made him.

She was aware of Dr Fletcher's ginger-haired appearance beside her and took a deep calming breath. She had to remember that she not only had to fool Dr Gareth Lacey himself, but also his contemporaries and colleagues. Nobody must realise she was Nemesis in their midst. A goddess of retribution.

'Ah, Gareth, I'd like to introduce you . . .' Just as they reached them, the round teddy-bear-like man moved slightly forward, revealing a dog collar. Davina blinked. What the hell . . . ? 'Gareth, meet Davina Granger. She's most anxious to talk shop.'

The tall, dark-haired man moved a pace forward.

She felt the nearness of him like the touch of a balmy breeze. The handsome face looked down at hers, his grey eyes fathomless, like a storm-tossed ocean, and as they moved over her, taking in the eyes, the mouth, the dress, they caressed her like a wave from the Atlantic.

She felt cold. But exhilarated. Drowning, but alive.

Davina felt the world around her give a strange kind of lurch. A weird tilt on its axis.

'Davina,' he said. And smiled.

The voice matched the eyes. There was the power of the ocean in that voice too. A fathomless tone that touched some part of her and set it quivering.

This was not good, Davina thought.

This was not good at all.

THREE

Alicia Norman arrived back at Oxford Station nearly five hours after leaving it, feeling cross, vaguely depressed, and just a little hurt.

She'd written to her mother last week to tell her she was coming back to the family home in Stratford-upon-Avon for the weekend. But when she'd arrived, it was to find that her father was in the Shetland Islands, interviewing a hermit-like author who'd agreed to give an interview for the first time in thirty years, and her mother in France, on a five-star cordon bleu cookery holiday. Even her brother, the country's leading drama critic, who had a self-contained studio at the large, sprawling Tudor mansion that was the Norman family residence, was in London to see the premiere of the latest glitzy musical.

Alicia had not been surprised so much as weary at the wasted journey. If only someone had phoned and let her know. Some homecoming!

It was nearly fully dark when she stepped through the main entrance to St Bede's and made her way to her room in Webster. Like most Oxford students, she'd probably 'live out' for her second year, taking rooms in town somewhere. She'd then be assigned another room in college for her final year, when exams would be sat.

As she made her way to her room on the top floor, she was already beginning to shrug off the disappointments of the day. To all outward appearances, Alicia Norman, with her wealthy, influential and literary-minded family, was an obvious candidate for Oxford, but she was also a shy girl, who still felt a bit wide-eyed and lost amid Oxford's cosmopolitan splendour. She had, however, found a good friend in the girl who was rooming next door to her, Emily White, a gregarious, outgoing girl from Newcastle-upon-Tyne.

Luckily for Alicia, Emily had very quickly seen through the charade of 'pretty little rich girl'. Recognising the shy dreamer underneath, she had automatically taken Alicia under her wing.

No sooner had Alicia got in and dumped her case on the floor than the door burst open behind her. The girl who erupted through it was tall, ginger-haired and wildly waving a hockey stick. Her watery blue eyes widened. 'Oh, it's you,' Emily panted. 'I thought you'd gone home for the weekend. When I heard someone moving about in here I thought you had burglars.'

Alicia laughed. 'I did go home for the weekend. But no one was there . . .' Her explanations trailed off as she spotted a movement behind her friend's shoulder in the open doorway. Her eyes widened, then she blushed. Vividly.

Emily had not been alone, it seemed. She'd always had a succession of boyfriends, which had at first surprised Alicia but now only amused her. Yet it still made her feel embarrassed about her own virginal state when Emily so obviously had the modern-woman scene down pat. And the latest of Emily's men was . . . well, frankly he was gorgeous.

Once again her eyes strayed to the stranger in the doorway, and Emily, spinning around, suddenly laughed. 'Oh. Right . . . er . . . ?'

'Jared.'

'Right, Jared. I forgot about you. Sorry, you must think I'm mad. When I bolted for the door like that. I mean, it's just that I knew no one should be in here, so I thought I'd come and investigate the noises.'

'So I gathered.' He stepped further into the room, shutting the door behind him, and his presence suddenly filled the small room. He was much taller than Alicia, who at only five feet four found most people towering over her. He had masses of nut-brown hair, which framed his head in wave after wave of healthily shining richness. His eyes were of a similar rich darkness. Like melting chocolate. His chin had a slight cleft.

Alicia felt her breath catch. Emily gave a swift double-take, looking from Jared to Alicia then Jared again, and began to grin, her freckles glowing. 'Alicia Norman, this is Jared . . . ?'

'Cowan.'

'Right. Jared just dropped by to ask if I'd be interested in helping him set up the Easter play.'

Alicia blinked blankly. Seeing her confusion, Jared shrugged and smiled. 'At the end of every Hilary Term the St Bede's Drama Group put on a play in the theatre. This year, for my sins, I've agreed to set it up. Somebody told me Emily here had had a bit of previous experience in theatre work, and since I needed all the help I could get . . .' He shrugged again, his eyes glued to Alicia's.

'Oh,' Alicia said, and Jared saw her glance at her friend nervously. She was everything he'd expected of her, seen close up, and more, and he could feel his heart start to thump in his chest. He sternly told himself not to be ridiculous.

She was way out of his league.

Jared had first spotted her last term, apparently along with the rest of the male population of St Bede's. It hadn't been hard to milk the grapevine for relevant details, and what he'd heard hadn't been encouraging. Her family was strictly top notch, with old-money connections and literary pretensions. For a working-class boy from Bicester, whose elder brother was currently in jail for burglary, and whose parents were frankly bewildered by their younger offspring's foray into the world of academia, it had not encouraged Jared to make any moves in her direction. He didn't need anyone looking down their nose at him. Even a nose as shapely as hers.

He'd been walking across the croquet lawns when he'd first seen her — hurrying through Becket Arch, dressed in the black-and-white ensemble known as subfusc. She'd been on her way to the first-year matriculation photograph session, which traditionally took place in the Fellows' Garden. Even at a distance, the long black hair streaming out behind her had caught his attention. Her eyes, he noticed now, were china blue, big and dark-lashed.

'I did a few plays at my old school,' Emily was saying brightly. 'The lead in the last one. You looking for a leading lady, Jared?' she teased, and Jared dragged his eyes away from Alicia. He looked vague for a moment, then he nodded.

'Leading lady, an assistant director, a writer, a props manager, painters, lighting engineers — you name it.'

Emily laughed. 'Never mind. You've got a while. It'll come together. You've put notices up?'

Jared nodded. 'I've got friends in the Engineering department who can help me with sound, lighting and so on, so that shouldn't be a problem.'

Emily, still shooting amused looks at her shell-shocked friend, suddenly snapped her fingers. 'Don't tell me! You're the J Cowan with those magical two letters after your name. The name I see every now and then on the notice boards?'

Alicia glanced at her friend, wondering how she could burble on so blithely and brightly, no doubt impressing their handsome visitor with her effervescent personality, when all she could do was stand there in tongue-tied silence, thinking how gorgeous he looked.

'Two magic letters?' Jared echoed, puzzled.

'Yes. E X. You are an exhibitioner, aren't you?'

He looked slightly embarrassed for a moment, then nodded.

Alicia was even more impressed. Every year, each school — be it English, History or Engineering — awarded its top two pupils a scholarship and an exhibition.

Brains as well as so much male beauty. It wasn't fair that some people seemed to have it all. She shook her head in bemusement and finally slipped off her coat, revealing a pale blue jumper of finest cashmere, and expensively tailored trousers. A fine gold chain hung round her neck. She pulled the silk scarf from her head, and as she did so masses of raven-sheened black hair cascaded down around her shoulders, reaching almost to her waist.

Emily watched Jared like a hawk, not missing the slight paling around his lips, the reflexive widening of his eyes, the sudden tenseness of his body. Oh yes! Emily fought back a sense of excitement. He was smitten! But he was also looking extremely wary.

It was not really surprising. The first day they'd met, Emily herself had been totally taken in by Alicia's chic clothes and unconscious air of breeding, and had thought dismally to herself that it was just her luck to be given a posh, stuck-up, literary toff from Stratford-upon-Avon for a neighbour. But as early as the second day, that opinion had been totally revised. Alicia might look like one thing, but was, underneath, totally another. Now, as she watched Jared Cowan take a few mental steps back, she cursed silently.

What her friend needed was a man in her life. A new start, not just in Oxford, but in her very way of thinking. And Jared Cowan was definitely attractive

'Well, I won't keep you any longer,' Jared said casually. 'Once I've got the production side lined up, I'll get back to you . . .'

'Hey, wait a minute,' Emily all but grabbed him as he turned to move away. 'We haven't even got anything settled yet. And if you're to have a play up and running by Easter, we have to get cracking.' And so do I, she thought gleefully. Getting these two together was going to be a cinch, once she got them over the first major hurdle. 'What play is it?'

she asked, deliberately walking over to the bed and bouncing down on it. She looked all set to stay till dinner time, when everyone dined in Hall at six sharp, and Alicia, for one, resigned herself to the inevitable.

'I don't know yet. I was hoping to get one specially written, but so far no one I've asked has seemed too keen, especially given how little time we have,' Jared admitted ruefully. 'But the library's stocked to the gills with Elizabethan dramas, so—'

Emily wrinkled her nose. 'Boring!' she interrupted, then shot up. 'I know! Alicia can write us one. Her brother must have taught her a thing or two about what makes for a good play. And didn't you tell me that you always wanted to write murder mysteries?' she shot at her friend, who was gaping at her, open-mouthed and appalled.

'Emily!' she squeaked. 'I can't write a play.'

Jared found his heart sinking at Alicia's protest, then told himself it was probably for the best. What, after all, did he have in common with a woman like her?

According to the gossip in the Junior Common Room, Alicia Norman was proving to be surprisingly elusive. Even the more upper-crust among them had met with little success when it came to bedding her. She'd turned down every date and overture she'd been offered. It had surprised a lot of the male contingent at St Bede's. Now, here he was, in the same room with her, and he could see why no man could possibly be good enough for her. She had it all — wealth, a powerful family, and her entry into the literary world. What could a man who wanted to build bridges and dams in all the remote corners of the world possibly offer her?

'Of course you can write a play!' Emily scoffed. 'What's to stop you?'

Alicia wished that Emily wouldn't do this. To Emily, nothing was impossible. To Alicia, the world felt like a minefield, something to be negotiated with care and caution so that she didn't get blown up. 'I've never written a play before in my life!' Alicia tried to explain. She glanced nervously at

Jared Cowan, who was watching her with a slightly puzzled expression in his deep, compelling eyes. She blinked, wondering if she was imagining the sensation of being pulled into those dark, dreamy depths.

'If you want to be a thriller writer, you're going to have to write a novel at some point,' Emily pointed out with unerring logic.

Alicia sighed. 'But, Emily, that's just a dream. I might love reading them, and solving the puzzle of the whodunit, taking in the atmosphere of classic country-house murders, but I could no more write one than fly to the moon.' Her frustration was palpable.

Emily's face took on a bulldog-like expression. 'Oh? And why not? You've certainly got the talent for it. I've read those short stories of yours, remember?'

Alicia felt as if she could strangle her. It wasn't like Emily to be so dense. 'And what do you think my aunt would say? Or Dad? Or Neville? They'd have a fit! A Norman, writing something so commercial as a whodunit! See sense, Emily.'

Jared, who'd been listening avidly, suddenly realised what her problem was. Neville Norman was a famous drama critic, an expert on George Bernard Shaw and Joe Orton. Her father owned a big literary magazine dedicated to fostering English Literature, and her aunt . . . ? Hadn't he overheard some disgruntled theologian talking about a feminist writer whose surname was Norman? Coming from that august family, no wonder Alicia would feel a bit wary penning something so plebeian as a murder mystery. But Jared loved murder mysteries. And his favourites, too, were the old classics.

'Alicia! For pity's sake! We're in a new millennium now!' Emily said scornfully, and Alicia blushed, feeling utterly humiliated. She knew that, compared to someone like Emily, she must seem like a veritable rabbit. But Emily hadn't grown up in a family where the written word was sacred. When other little girls had been read tales of Beatrix Potter or gone with Alice through the Looking Glass, Graeme Norman had read to his daughter Melville, Thackeray, Chaucer and Wordsworth.

Emily, seeing the shy, hurt tide of colour wash over Alicia's delicate skin, could have kicked herself for her thoughtlessness. 'Oh hell, Alicia, I'm sorry,' she said contritely, getting off the bed and coming to her side, giving her drooping shoulders a comforting bear hug. 'But sometimes I could shake you. You'd write great murder mysteries. And if you really want to do it, surely your family will understand?'

Alicia gave her a speaking look. Emily laughed. OK, so they wouldn't. But she wasn't about to give up. She looked across at Jared, who was once more looking at Alicia with an appraising eye. She understood it at once, of course. He was already beginning to see that, with Alicia, what you saw was definitely not what you got. Which boded well. Some men could be so dense.

Jared was indeed wondering why someone who seemed to have it all sounded as lost as he had sometimes felt himself.

All his life, he'd had a fascination for engineering, ever since his first construction kit at the age of eight. His father worked in a shoe shop. His mother was a home help. His brother, unemployed since he'd left school, had simply fallen into thieving, along with several of his mates. Jared, doing so well in mathematics and the sciences at school, had always been the cuckoo in the Cowan nest. Going on to Oxford had only made him even more of an outsider. Oh, his parents had been overjoyed, fearing he might go the same way as Kevin, and grateful that he'd channelled his energies into his studies. But they didn't understand him. It had never occurred to him that Alicia Norman, with her beauty, upper-class superiority, wealth and influence, could be in a similar position.

'Look, there's no reason you can't help Jared here out of a jam, is there?' Emily asked craftily. 'We can at least toss a few ideas around. Get him started? Hmm?'

Alicia shot Jared an agonised look. His dark eyes softened, and he wanted to respond instantly to that unspoken appeal for help. But then his eyes flicked across to Emily. And some strange, silent communication seemed to pass between them.

Jared took a deep breath. One part of his mind warned him he was walking straight into quicksand. Another part cheered him on. 'Well, I would be grateful for a bit of help,' he began cautiously. 'And a contemporary, original play would be . . . well, a bit of a feather in everyone's cap. Including yours. Your tutors would be pleased.'

'See? And who wouldn't want to keep Dr Lacey happy. What a hunk he is!' Emily crowed. 'I've always envied you, being taught by him, Alicia.'

Emily steered her to her desk and dragged out some paper.

'Well?' Alicia said helplessly. 'What am I supposed to do now? I can't just snap my fingers and come up with a plot!'

Jared moved to take the other chair beside the desk. He turned it around and straddled it, dangling his arms over the back, and then ran one hand through his shock of thick, dark hair, causing Alicia to catch her breath. He was wearing an old shirt that was frayed at the cuffs, and jeans so faded they were almost white. He was so unlike the men she was used to.

'I'm no expert,' Jared began softly, 'but aren't some things in murder mysteries pretty basic?'

Alicia was fascinated by his voice. It held no nasal upper-crust drawl. No pretentiousness. No accent at all, in fact. It was just a wonderful voice — strong, masculine, warm.

'We need a killer, don't we?' Jared said, watching her closely. Partly because he was wary now of scaring her, sensing her vulnerability. And partly because he could look at those china-blue eyes all day long. For much, much longer, in fact . . .

'Oh. Yes, of course we need a killer,' Alicia said, blushing furiously. What an idiot he must think her! 'And a victim. And a motive. And between four or five suspects, a few red herrings and . . .' She trailed off. In her mind's eye she could see her brother's sneering face. He would regard a classic murder mystery as being a light-as-air irrelevance.

'Perhaps,' she said slowly, 'we could make it meaningful in some way?'

29

Emily began to shoot forward, sensing danger signs, but Jared shot her a 'back off' look. Such was Emily's instinctive confidence in him that she found herself — most unusually — obeying him. 'OK. We are doing this for the St Bede's Easter play after all, so it wouldn't hurt us to put in a bit of relevant social content.'

Jared, oh, Jared, I could kiss you, Emily thought. If you weren't so smitten with Alicia, that is!

'We could centre the play around a family home,' Alicia said. 'Perhaps in a run-down area?'

Jared leaned forward, propping his chin up on his clenched fist. It brought him to within inches of her. Alicia felt her breath catch again. She could actually see the tiny pores in his skin. The shadow of a beard on his jaw. If she ran her finger across his chin, she would feel the tiny prickles scratch her . . .

'You want to go down the domestic violence route?' he hazarded, looking into her eyes. She blushed, and quickly looked away. And once again, a strange, thoughtful, but glowingly tender look crossed his face.

'Yes, but not a husband-wife murder. That's too pat. Why not give it a twist?' she murmured thoughtfully, her eyes glowing now as she got the bit between her teeth. 'Why not make it a case of a parent being battered by a child? The mother could be the victim, and she could have a son — a teenage son. Big for his age.'

'A fifteen-year-old perhaps?' Emily put in her penny's worth. 'They can be big and brutal at that age.'

'Right! He could be angry with his mother for some rea-son — confused. She's having an affair, and he's found out.'

'So the husband would be one of our suspects, right?' Jared prompted, getting into the swing of it too.

'Of course!' Alicia said, reaching for the paper and beginning to jot down notes. Over her bent head, Emily and Jared once more passed a silent message to each other.

'But I'm not going to write the play itself, remember?' Alicia said, her notes finished, her burst of happiness and confidence diminishing.

'No, of course not,' Emily murmured, her eyes twinkling.

'Right,' Jared said, his eyes dropping once more to the lovely profile of the woman next to him. Her skin was as creamy white as a camellia. Her long black hair was so close, he itched to stroke it, to run his fingers through the silken length. She was tapping a pen thoughtfully against her lips; lips that were coated with a sheen of no doubt very expensive lipstick. Her mother, he thought, would have taught her how to dress and don make-up before she hit her teens. He wanted to kiss that expensive lipstick from her mouth . . .

'And the son will be the obvious suspect, though of course he isn't the murderer,' Alicia was saying happily. 'We'll have to plant a really incriminating piece of evidence on him. But what we need is an outsider.'

Emily caught sight of her watch and yelped. 'Hell! It's nearly six! Come on, let's get to Hall or we'll be stuck in the queue for ages. I hear we've got some bigwig dining with us tonight, a woman poet. I heard a couple of third-year Lit students going on about her. Apparently, there's to be a big announcement at dinner.'

And suddenly Alicia remembered catching sight of Davina Granger on the train. Her family would expect her to cultivate the poet's friendship, of course. She looked up into dark eyes that were watching her with such a strange, gentle intensity, and her breath caught again.

If she was to help him with this play he'd agreed to put on, she was going to be seeing a lot more of Jared Cowan.

Jared smiled, stood up, and offered his elbow. 'Would you care to join me for dinner?'

The shirt had a hole in it, and she could see the point of his elbow peeking through.

Feeling a right idiot, but also a warm glow of pleasure bathing her from head to toe, she rose. Regally, she inclined her head. 'Thank you, yes I would.'

And together, much to Emily's amusement, they left, arm in arm, to walk across the dark, rain-sodden lawns to Hall.

FOUR

The Hall was already crowded and extremely noisy when the principal and his party arrived. As Sin-Jun very gallantly escorted Davina to the High Table, where scouts delivered meals for them, there was a just a slight drop in the noise level. The female students, according to their natures, were either intrigued and approving of her shorn locks and fashionable dress, or were scornful and envious.

Davina, not sure whether to be relieved or annoyed at the seating arrangement, found that Dr Gareth Lacey had been seated directly on her left.

'I hope you won't find the food too homely for you, m'dear,' Sin-Jun said. 'Chef isn't always able to be as creative as he would like and still keep to his budget.'

Davina smiled, said she was sure it would be delicious, and took her pick of the two options on the day's menu.

'So, where do you think you'll start?' Sin-Jun said, and Davina nearly jumped out of her skin. For one blank-minded second she thought he was asking where she was going to start in her campaign to destroy his English literary don. The hand holding her fork, which bore the St Bede's crest of arms on the handle, shook alarmingly.

'Sorry?' she squeaked, then cleared her voice. 'Sorry? Start where?'

'With the anthology?' Gareth said quietly, sensing her confusion. His stormy-grey eyes watched her with a slightly puzzled, gentle look. She was obviously nervous. He wouldn't have thought a poet of her reputation would be overawed by Oxford, but she obviously was. He realised, of course, that with no formal education to speak of, some people felt at a very great disadvantage when they were surrounded by so many academically successful people, but he hadn't expected this woman to be prone to such feelings. She looked too confident, too self-sufficient. Obviously, he was wrong.

Davina sighed in sudden relief. The anthology! She took a deep breath. 'Well, my publishers want me to pick a hundred or so of my favourite modern verses, including at least twenty different poets and from as many different countries as I can manage. Then there's the foreword. I think the foreword will have to be the last project — I can hardly write an introduction explaining the choice of poems before I've decided which ones I'm going to choose.'

Sin-Jun nodded, but already his mind was wandering. What he knew about poetry could be written on the back of a postage stamp. What he was really interested in was boosting the science departments within the college. Young Jared Cowan, whom he could see seated at the first table down, was where the future of St Bede's lay.

'So do you have any idea where you want to start?' Gareth, recognising the look in the principal's eye which meant that Sin-Jun was off on one of his mental rambles, was more than happy to take over the job of looking after their guest.

'I thought I'd start with the Irish poets first,' Davina said, turning to look Gareth full in the face. She'd been avoiding doing so ever since that first meeting in the SCR.

To think, now, that she'd thought Rex Jimson-Clarke was her quarry!

If only he was, a taunting, panicking voice piped up in the back of her mind. It would be so much easier. For she was already falling prey to those damned grey eyes again. They were truly fathomless, full of intriguing darts of expression.

Gareth smiled. It transformed a face already way too handsome for its own good into a breath-taking one. Or rather, for *my* own good, she thought wryly. 'That's always a good place to start,' he agreed. 'I have the latest Seamus Heaney, if you'd like to borrow it.'

Davina nodded and murmured her thanks.

She knew herself well enough to recognise all the signs of attraction, but never before had the feeling been so strong. So instant. So physical. So primordial.

'And after the Irish?' Gareth probed delicately.

'The Americans.'

'You should check out the Caribbean too.'

Davina nodded, but didn't elaborate. Let him think she needed guidance. The more he thought it, the more he'd offer it. The more she'd take it. The closer she could get to him.

You should be thinking of running, not getting closer.

The thought was so loud it almost sounded like an extra voice in her head. It made her jump. Grimly she ignored the warning. So she was attracted to him. So what? She'd been attracted to men before and said 'no'. Just because her body wanted him didn't mean she had to allow her mind or her heart to follow suit. She was thirty years old, for pity's sake. She was in control. Of course she was! Besides, getting close to him was all part of the plan, she reminded herself.

'What kind of poetry are you going to be looking for? And are you going to include any of your own?' Gareth found himself leaning towards her, eager for any words that might fall from those full lips.

When he'd first set eyes on her in the SCR, nothing had prepared him for the vision in lilac and silver walking towards him. The touch of those huge, cat-green eyes on his face. The sheer power of the woman — even the way she moved had called to his mind visions of a stalking tigress. His body, even now, was quivering in tension at her nearness. A tingling anticipation in his nerve endings. He hadn't felt anything like it since . . . well, since he'd met Martine, his late wife.

Then he'd been eighteen, and it had been love at first sight. Now . . . now he was a mature man of thirty-eight, not a hormone-ridden teenager. He shouldn't be feeling this level of sexual awareness. It was . . . well, it should have been embarrassing, but, Gareth realised, with a start of nervous surprise, he didn't feel the least embarrassed. Excited, yes. Bewildered, OK. But she was also looking at him with those interested, cat-green eyes, and he knew that if she was feeling even anything remotely the same, he was going to have another woman seriously in his life for the first time in nearly sixteen years.

Another love. It was a staggering thought. Especially given they'd only just met.

When he'd got up that morning, he'd had no inkling that his life was never going to be the same again. And that was terrifying.

'Yes, I thought that I'd write a new poem, expressly for the anthology,' she said, exciting his brain now.

'Oh? What topic?'

'I'm not sure. When I first got here a little plaque told me I was in St Agatha Quad. I couldn't remember who she was, but I thought, in honour of St Bede's, I might write a modern-day version of her story.'

Gareth felt his mind racing. What an idea! With her vivid, sometimes shattering gift of prose, a modern rendition of St Agatha would be . . .

'Do you know her life story?' Davina asked, seeing those grey eyes glow. He really was passionate about poetry, she realised with a strange, tender yet savage lurch of her heart. That wasn't fair. In her mind's eye, she'd always pictured Dr Gareth Lacey as a burned-out don, a man who'd tried and failed to write poetry, and had been warped and embittered by his failure. A man going through the motions, tutoring pupils out of a desire to hold on to his cushy job, rather than out of any real desire to impart knowledge or endow a love of poetry.

But that was so obviously not the case with this man that she felt, once again, that sudden shifting inside her. The mental equivalent of stepping down, expecting to find a rung of the ladder beneath you, only to encounter thin air instead. Damn him, why couldn't he just fit in with her image of him?

'I don't think much of her life history has ever been recorded,' he said thoughtfully, dragging her back to their conversation. 'I know that St Agatha, the one our quad is named after at least, was also better known as St Agnes. I think one of Rex's fellow theologians might be able to tell you all that's known about her. The only thing I can remember about her is that she was one of those child martyrs. I seem to recall that she died around the turn of the fourth century and was beheaded for refusing to marry.'

Davina, who'd been about to take a sip of the excellent Veuve Clicquot that Sin-Jun had ordered from the college cellars for the occasion, found herself pausing. A rather dreamy smile crossed her face. She slowly nodded her head. 'Now there's a poem in the making.'

Gareth nodded. 'In the style of "Leaf-Churning, Eye-Balling"?' He named one of her earlier, extremely controversial poems. It was a good choice. She, too, had been thinking of that irreverent, shocking style of prose herself, as he'd been telling her about St Agnes. Or St Agatha. And, once again, she felt her heart lurch.

He's reading my mind!

His sensitivity, the very synchronicity of their thoughts, made her feel as panic-stricken as she'd ever been in her life. No! They just couldn't be on the same wavelength like this. It was not fair! He was her enemy, not her soul mate! Dammit. Think of something else. Quick! Anything. 'Isn't there a day of the year called St Agnes' Eve?' she asked, her voice as weak as the feeling in her knees.

'That's right. Sometime in January, I think. According to legend, a woman will dream of her future husband on that night.'

Davina managed a rather bitter laugh. 'That doesn't seem very appropriate, considering poor St Agnes' fate.'

Gareth smiled. 'No. Perhaps not.'

'Well, if I don't write about Agnes, perhaps I'll include the poem I'm working on now. It's called "The Flame Moth".'

She felt safer, and much happier, now they were on her home territory. But she made a mental note to herself: this man has hidden depths. Make sure you don't stumble into one of them, girl.

Gareth, his lasagne cold and forgotten on his plate, found himself leaning even closer to her. The rapt look on his face was being monitored not only by those undergraduates seated near enough to High Table to be able to see it, but also by his fellow academics. He looked enthralled. Enraptured. But when academic ears tuned discreetly in, it was to find them talking about anthologies, old martyred saints, and poetry. Nothing at all exciting, such as life with a Hollywood star, or the sexual meaning behind some of her more erotic poems. Perhaps, after all, they mused, Gareth was playing true to form, even with the exotically beautiful Davina Granger. For, of all St Bede's many venerable, respected fellows, Dr Gareth Lacey was considered to be one of the most dedicated. His vast knowledge of the Romantics, as well as the moderns, was almost legendary. And in a town like Oxford, that was an accolade indeed. Most people put it down to the fact that he had been widowed so early.

He'd married at the age of twenty, just before sitting finals. But then, barely two years later, he'd returned to their digs one day to find his wife dead, slumped on the sofa. An unsuspected and undetected heart condition had given her a massive coronary.

For the first five years after her death, it had been obvious to everyone that Gareth hadn't even thought about other women. Drawn to his tragedy, his love of the Romantic poets, his good looks, status, and distinctive male 'something', many female students had tried to seduce him out of his celibacy. To the college's extreme collective relief, none of them had ever succeeded. For the past ten years, Gareth had occasionally been seen with other women, but nothing serious.

Now, Rex Jimson-Clarke, who was watching the two of them, rather hoped that Davina Granger was going to be the one to waken the sleeping prince. Gareth was still too young to slide into crusty bachelordom.

'"The Flame Moth",' Gareth murmured now, rolling the words around his mouth, savouring the erotic image it conveyed. 'A love poem?'

'What else burns quite like love?' Davina said drolly.

Gareth gave a quick grimace. 'Yes.'

Davina, once again about to take a sip of the exquisite wine, looked at him sharply instead. 'You sound as if you know,' she said quietly.

'I do. I lost my wife when I was twenty-two.'

Davina inclined her head gently in understanding. 'She's been gone a long time now,' she said softly, warily, choosing her words with care.

Gareth nodded. 'Yes. Raw pain fades to sad memory.'

He has a way with words, Davina thought with a pang. Just like me. No! Dammit, she was doing it again.

At least it was obvious that he was over his wife's loss. It was one thing to kick a man when he was up and fighting, another thing altogether to kick him when he was down. No. Gareth Lacey was still fair game.

'So, how far have you got with the new poem?' he asked, fascinated by the fleeting ripples of expression crossing her face. For those few seconds back there, when she'd been so lost in thought, he'd detected savagery, compassion, and decision marching across her eyes. He knew, without being told, that the world inside this woman's head would be a land of extremes. And it was a land he longed to explore. She was the most outrageous, dangerous, fascinating creature in the world. And, although common sense told him it would be wiser to stay away, Gareth had never been a great believer in that commodity.

He was an emotions man himself.

'Oh, I've just got a basic outline of the poem at the moment,' she admitted easily. 'A few thoughts. A line or two.'

Gareth nodded. 'Are you like an artist who can't stand to have anybody watch her paint or see the painting till it's done?' he asked anxiously.

Davina was. But for tonight's purposes, things would be different. She could feel how strongly he was willing her to say no. She shrugged one elegant shoulder. 'No, I don't mind talking about it at all,' she lied with a bright, devastating smile. 'The concept is love as the great deceiver. For centuries poets have regarded it as the ultimate goal. The reason for which mankind was created. The great excuse for murder, insanity, and self-destruction. The Flame Moth is a woman—'

'You don't think men get their wings singed as well?' he interrupted, challenging her without fear.

'Not so many, and not so often,' Davina responded firmly.

Gareth, much to her surprise, thought about that, then slowly nodded his head. 'Perhaps that's true. Many men, psychologically, have a certain protection.'

'But not you,' Davina thought, then realised, when he started and threw her an astonished look, that she'd actually spoken the thought out loud.

Too late to take it back now. She looked at him with steady green eyes. Gareth felt his breath catching. It had been an outrageous thing to say to a man she'd known less than an hour. But she was spot on. He shrugged. 'Perhaps. I suppose living and breathing the Romantic poets for the majority of my life has caused my hard shell to be rubbed away.'

Davina felt like crying. Damn him, he was doing it again. Undermining her. Where was the swaggering bully

David's letters had conjured up so vividly? Where was the bitter, twisted man who could drive one of his students to suicide?

Obviously, he was a far more complex character than she'd ever imagined. A mass of contradictions, human failings, human majesties . . . just like herself. No! No, she must not keep linking them together like this. He was the enemy!

She reached for her wine and this time took a hearty gulp. It didn't seem to help much.

'So, you have a Flame Moth . . .' he prompted, eager to steer the conversation away from such soul-scraping intimacy. Although he already knew, in his heart of hearts, that they were destined to become lovers, set on some pre-determined course, it didn't mean that he had to rush ahead like a blind, stumbling fool.

'Yes.' Davina dragged in a wavering breath, forcing her mind to concentrate. 'A moth who learns that "Love is a flame for gossamer-minded fools . . ." And that's the only line I've written so far!' She laughed, a bit nervously, showing that she, too, was not quite so comfortable with heart-shattering revelations as she might appear.

Gareth leaned back, both physically and mentally. Time to come up for air. And did he need it! His heart was thundering so hard in his chest he felt as though he'd just swum a mile under water.

As if sensing the sudden change in atmosphere, Sin-Jun chose that moment to rise. 'Ladies and gentlemen of St Bede's,' he bellowed, to sudden silence. Fluently he went on to introduce Davina, explaining her honorary status for the duration of Hilary Term, her commission to edit the anthology, and his hope that the English Literature students would attend the lecture she'd agreed to give on 22 April. There was the expected enthusiastic round of applause.

Seated at her table beside Jared, Alicia especially felt a rush of heady excitement. Once she told her father that Davina was at St Bede's, he was bound to come down, hoping to wangle an interview with her. She wrote such powerful, awe-inspiring, sometimes frightening poetry. If only Alicia could get up the nerve to speak to her. But that night, after dinner had finished, the poetess was quickly surrounded by avid students, so she and Jared left early, she to write up her notes on the play, he to revise for his finals.

Finally, nearing midnight, Davina managed to escape Hall. It seemed to Gareth that she left an ominous feeling of emptiness in her wake.

As she walked through the semi-lit darkness of the college, through Becket Arch and across the lawns, she paused to stare down at the pond. A light was on in the library — some poor soul burning the midnight oil no doubt — and it cast just enough light on the pond for her to see the ponderous turning of a black-edged fin. Did fish sleep, she wondered? And imagined a poem where she was a fish, never sleeping, turning endlessly in a pond that never grew any bigger . . . Restlessly, she turned the poem off, and walked to her new rooms, undressing and stripping off with a leaden-limbed weariness that had her tumbling into bed in exhaustion.

But, such is the way of things, once she'd done so, she quickly discovered that sleep was suddenly a million miles away. Instead, she lay in the unfamiliar bed, looking at the ceiling, thinking of him. Gareth Lacey. She found herself cataloguing him, listing the ways in which he was so different from what she'd expected. He was young, not old. Good-looking, not ugly. Sensitive. Clever. Passionate about poetry. Lovely eyes. Lovely voice. And he understood her.

She tossed violently on the bed, not liking that last thought at all. In her rehearsals for how things would go, she'd pictured herself as a Mata-Hari-type figure, wrapping a happy, smitten, panting Dr Lacey around her little finger.

He might be feeling happy right now. Even a man with no sensitivity at all wouldn't have been able to miss the strong sexual signals she'd been giving out. And he might be smitten. She was a big enough girl to know what a dark, deepening look in a man's eyes meant. But she'd seen no sign of panting. And certainly no sign of a willingness to be wrapped around her little finger. She tossed again. Dammit, this was no good. Young or old, good-looking or not, he was still the enemy.

OK. So, as things stood, it was beginning to look as if she wouldn't be able to entice him into her orbit, make him want her, perhaps even love her, and then flit away again without getting her own wings singed a bit. All right. She could cope with that. She just had to concentrate on her two goals.

Dr Gareth Lacey had betrayed the student/tutor trust, and for that he would know how it felt to be betrayed himself. He was going to fall in love with her, dammit, just so that she could throw that love right back in his face. Even if she had to cut out her own heart to do it.

But Dr Gareth Lacey had also driven her brother to suicide by labelling him a cheat and having him sent down from his beloved Oxford. And for that, he, too, would be labelled a cheat. He, too, would be sent down from Oxford, kicked out by his college and ostracised by the university.

Tonight, she'd begun step one.

Tomorrow, she would figure out a way to accomplish step two.

FIVE

By her third week in Oxford, Davina was becoming desperate. She'd talked to practically everyone in college who knew Gareth Lacey personally, right down to the scouts who cleaned his rooms, but nobody had a bad word to say about the man. She'd managed to pump both the other English dons for every little titbit concerning him, from the strictly professional to the downright personal. But nothing.

The scouts came up with such facts as that he didn't smoke, liked his coffee with cream and one sugar, always folded his clothes neatly, and shaved with a wet razor. Very helpful!

The undergraduates were easier to get gossiping about possible scandals, but even they were of little help, and Davina was getting heartily sick of all the adoration the man inspired. Why couldn't they see through him?

For some reason, she was never able to bring herself to steer the talk around to David. But if she had, she had no doubts everyone would roundly lecture her on how it was not poor Dr Lacey's fault. And that, Davina simply could not bear.

Her shoulders were unconsciously slumped with dejection as she crossed Wallace Quad. She was going to the

Bodleian Library, the world-famous institution, one of the oldest libraries in Europe. But even that thought could not cheer her. Still, like it or not, it was time she made further progress on the anthology. She'd been the one to bully her publishers into supporting the idea, knowing she needed an 'in' at Oxford. Now she was stuck with it.

The last of February's cruel wind teased her flapping blue coat as she trudged along. She had to find a way to get to the man. But how? He seemed to have everybody fooled.

She almost bumped into a tall, elegantly dressed man as he stepped through the main gates. 'Miss Granger! I had no idea you were in Oxford. Neville Norman,' Alicia's brother introduced himself.

Davina smiled politely at the theatre critic. Neville Norman's reviews usually demonstrated that he knew what he was talking about, and he was one of the few critics who could actually give constructive criticism, but she was in no mood for idle chat, and quickly excused herself.

Neville ambled his way towards Webster, but his sister was not in. It didn't take him long to discover from a third-year Theology student down the hall that Alicia Norman was to be found in the theatre nowadays. She was writing the Easter play. This startling news both amused and annoyed him. Why hadn't she written and told them all about it?

The theatre held a modest one hundred seats, but it was well appointed, the stage simple but adequate. At the moment only the stage was lit, and Neville was able to creep silently forward, unseen and unheard, and take a seat just a few rows back from centre stage.

He'd caught them, it seemed, mid-audition. Even as he watched, the good-looking man next to Alicia gave a plea for quiet.

Alicia, her ever-present notebook in her hand, looked up and smiled. She was glad Jared was in charge of casting the play — the whining and wheedling pleas for inclusion just seemed to roll from his shoulders like water off a duck's back.

'Right, we're casting the heroine first,' his strong voice easily carried to the back of the theatre. 'She's the murder victim, the wife and battered mother. You've all read the excellent character analysis provided by our august and astute author here . . .' he turned and bowed deeply at Alicia, who blushed hotly. Clown!

In his seat, Neville found himself stiffening. This play sounded suspiciously like a cheesy whodunit to him.

'You're all supplied with dialogue from Act Two, Scene One,' Jared continued smoothly. 'Right, Vera. You first.'

Neville wasn't sure he was ready to listen to words penned by his own sister. What if they were corny? But they weren't. The scene Vera performed was a straightforward but touching scene between the heroine and an as yet unseen boy, her son, who was challenging his mother about an affair she was having. And as the scene progressed, it was obvious to Neville that the scene was going to be some kind of catalyst. Neville, in instinctive critic mode, began to make notes.

'Right, thank you everybody,' Jared said, after the last audition had finished. 'If you can just wait a moment . . .' He went back to consult with Alicia, but Neville already knew that there was only one possible choice. The ginger-haired girl had been by far the best.

'Well, what do you think?' Alicia whispered to Jared anxiously. 'I think Emily was good, don't you?' But would the others think Alicia was only recommending her because of their friendship?

Jared could see the worry in those big, china-blue eyes and grinned widely. 'I agree.' His eyes were tender as he watched her face light up. She was really coming out of her shell now. These last few weeks had been the best of his life, watching the butterfly emerge from the chrysalis.

They picked the best actresses for the other two parts. All of them were members of OUDS, the Oxford University Drama Society, and already had experience.

Alicia sighed. Things were happening so fast! Just three weeks ago she'd never even heard of Jared Cowan or thought about the St Bede's Easter play. Now, here she was, actually writing it and watching it as it took shape. And all done with Jared right beside her.

In his seat, Neville wondered what his aunt Georgina would say about all this. Any pride she might have in her niece following in her literary footsteps was bound to be dented when she learned Alicia was writing a dismal who-dunit. For the woman who'd won the Booker Prize for a scathing indictment of sexual inequality in modern Britain, it would be a come-down. And as for his dad . . . ? Neville shook his head. What on earth had made her agree to such a thing?

He simply had to nip this thing in the bud now, before it got any further. He walked purposely forward, still, at that moment, unnoticed.

'Right, now we've got the ladies sorted,' Jared called out cheerfully, 'lead on with the men.' There was a ribald series of catcalls, comments and swaggers, as a group of male under-graduates shuffled on to the stage.

'For you miserable-looking lot, we have a first-draft scene from Act One. We're casting for the killer, the victim's husband, and the detective.'

Alicia made a sudden sound. Jared turned and looked at her.

'What?' he asked softly.

'I was just thinking,' Alicia said. 'What if we make the detective a woman? Nowadays a senior police officer is just as likely to be a woman. She could even have marriage problems of her own.'

She was sitting in a folding chair and Jared put one knee on the floor in front of her to get more comfortable. As he did so, his loose-fitting, open-necked shirt gaped open, allowing her to see the strong column of his throat and the warm and smooth, tanned expanse of his almost hairless chest.

Alicia dragged in a ragged breath, pulling her eyes away. Jared noticed, and felt his body heat, as though an invisible sun had suddenly come out. He felt his nipples harden, beginning to throb as he imagined her touching them, her white, gentle fingers moving over his body . . .

Alicia swallowed. She licked lips gone suddenly dry, unaware of how the flickering of her tongue tip was driving him crazy. It was hard for her to breathe, let alone think, when he was kneeling before her like that. Like an old-fashioned swain about to propose.

'Are we going to be here all day, Jared, or what?' one of the male students on the stage called restlessly. Jared turned and made a nicely judged rude gesture. Everyone erupted into laughter.

'We'll discuss it tonight, after Hall. Come to my place?' Jared whispered quickly. He had a room in Wolsey.

She nodded, blushing, thinking about being alone with him in his room. 'OK.'

Jared turned, saw Neville, took in the Savile Row suit, the ginger hair and rolled umbrella, and hesitated. It didn't take a genius to know that this was no undergraduate. 'Can I help you, mate?' Jared asked genially, getting up lithely.

Alicia, along with everyone else, turned to see who he was talking to, and felt the blood drain from her face.

'I was looking for my sister,' Neville said smoothly. 'I was told she was here.'

Jared glanced automatically at the gaggle of female undergraduates, but it was from behind him that he heard a response. 'Neville! What are you doing here?' Alicia croaked.

And suddenly, there was a surprising tension in the room.

Neville ignored his sister's dismay. 'I just thought I'd come by and see how you were doing,' he said easily. 'I had no idea you were writing a play,' he added mildly. But his level, gleaming brown eyes seemed to bore into hers, and she felt herself go a whiter shade of pale.

Jared, sensing some kind of problem, moved restlessly. 'It's a wonderful play she's written for us, Mr Norman,' he came to Alicia's defence instantly, and heard the others around him murmur in agreement.

'Hmm,' Neville said noncommittally. 'I was listening in. It sounded to me,' he laughed jovially, 'like a "whodunit".'

Jared stiffened, sensing the put-down in his voice. 'It is a whodunit,' he said, deliberately cheerfully. 'With a complex victim, a fallibly human killer, a good smattering of hearty red herrings and plenty of clever clues. It's also set on a run-down estate, rife with crime, and has a lot to say about domestic violence, a woman's right to happiness and the repercussions of the twin urges to love and to kill.'

The students around him nodded in enthusiastic agreement, but, naturally enough, most of their attention was centred on Neville Norman himself. It wasn't often that anyone got to meet a real lion of the theatre.

'Indeed?' Neville said coldly. He didn't like the challenging look in the younger man's eyes. He didn't like the way Alicia moved closer to him, as if for protection. And he especially didn't like the way he must have lured his sister into writing this trashy little play either.

'In that case,' Neville smiled wolfishly, 'perhaps I can request an invitation to the opening night? Even review it for you in the local press?'

There was a sudden collective whoosh of caught breath followed by a whoop of delight as the others considered their huge luck. To be cast in such an obscure play, and only to have their efforts reviewed by the great Neville Norman!

Jared sensed trouble, but what could he do? Old Sin-Jun would jump for joy to have St Bede's so honoured. So would the English Literature tutors. He could hardly say No. Although, from the agonised look in Alicia's eyes, he longed to do so. Perhaps he could put him off? 'Thank you, Mr Norman. But the play only goes out for the one night. I don't know if you'll be free. It's on April the second.'

Neville made a great show of opening his diary. 'It's a date.'

Aware that now was not the time to tackle him, Alicia turned away helplessly.

'Please, do carry on with the auditions,' Neville said urbanely, and took a seat next to his sister.

Reluctantly, Jared restored order and began to call up the men for audition. Not surprisingly, with the great Neville Norman watching their every clumsy, amateurish move, there was a lot of spluttering and fluffing of lines, stiff acting and nervous coughing. Jared, trying to see through the nervousness to detect any real talent underneath, found that the *joie de vivre* had gone right out of the day. Alicia looked as tense as a violin string.

'OK, Rupert Greyling-Simms,' he called wearily.

By her side, Neville suddenly perked up. With a name like that, the tall handsome blond man who stepped on stage had to be a relation to Seymour Greyling-Simms, otherwise known as the Earl of Warrington. The family had a huge ancestral pile not far from Stratford-upon-Avon. Of course, he'd never met the Earl — they moved in very different circles.

As the blond man accepted the pages of script from his sweating predecessor, Neville noted the strong family resemblance. The son, then. Heir to title and estate?

Then the critic in him took over. The boy had a good voice. Upper-crust, but clear. The role he was reading was that of Sam Blake, the lover and eventual killer of the victim. And he was good. Neville, who'd reviewed most of the great actors of the day, recognised at once that highly strung, volatile nature that all the best actors possessed.

On the stage, Rupert Greyling-Simms was pleading with his invisible lover to leave her husband and children and get off the estate. He was offering her all that he had, and the desperation of the character was coming through clearly.

Nor was Neville the only one to recognise the man's talent. Jared and Emily were both on the edge of their seats, and even the other waiting undergraduates were nodding at each other, silently acknowledging the fact that Rupert was the best so far.

An hour later, and the play was cast. Neville, despite pointed hints by Jared, had not left, but stuck close to his sister's side.

Rupert Greyling-Simms hovered on the edge of the stage, half in darkness, half in light, looking at no one but Alicia. He hadn't been able to take his eyes off her from the moment he'd walked into the theatre. He'd seen the auditions for the play advertised last week, and had decided to go along, more out of a sense of defiance than anything else. He knew his father had no time for the arts, but acting was something Rupert had always been good at, and he knew he could join the college play without too much flak from his family.

From the moment he'd stepped into the theatre and seen her, he knew he simply had to win a role in the play. Any role. She was like a . . . a vision. Those raven tresses. Those amazing, wide blue eyes. Skin like a camellia. And shy too. He'd watched those blushes, that downward sweep of long eyelashes, that defensive body posture. Enchanting. Utterly enchanting. She stood out from the other women, like a fresh, innocent daisy in a field of Venus flytraps.

He'd longed to go over and speak to her, but that damned Jared Cowan was always fawning all over her. Kneeling down in front of her, whispering, laughing. But he'd got a lucky break with the arrival of her brother. It had put his rivals into a spin, putting them off their stride. Rupert was impressed by nobody, apart from his father, and that lack of nervousness had allowed him to shine on stage. Now, seeing that Jared was at last talking to that ginger-haired stick insect who was to be his leading lady, he made his move.

The first Alicia was aware of him was when her brother suddenly stiffened, an odd, uncharacteristically fawning expression crossing his face. She turned and saw the handsome man they'd cast as Sam Blake coming towards her.

'Alicia,' Rupert said softly, smiling. 'I hope you don't mind first names. Particularly as we're going to be working so closely together?'

'No, of course not,' Alicia said, a bit flustered.

'My Lord?' Neville said, formally offering his hand. 'Your father is the Earl of Warrington, isn't he?' he added.

'That's right. But here at Oxford . . .' Rupert shrugged off his title with becoming modesty and Neville smiled.

'I understand. And congratulations in landing the leading part.'

This of course, Neville thought instantly, changed things. When you had an earl's son in the play then of course Alicia must continue to be associated with it.

'Alicia, I really like the part of Sam Blake,' Rupert said, feeling himself shudder as those blue eyes turned his way. They really were superb eyes. Aphrodite must have had eyes like these, he thought dazedly.

'Oh,' Alicia murmured, not sure what else to say.

'I'm sure the rest of the lines you'll give him will be as good as those I read today. I was really impressed with the play,' he added softly, and she rewarded him with yet another look from those blue eyes. And this time . . . yes, a slight smile. Rupert felt like the luckiest mortal on earth. She was exquisite. Divine. Just what he was looking for.

Neville recognised at once the look in those noble brown eyes and smiled. Of course, it was ridiculous to hope for too much so soon. But still . . . Rupert was obviously smitten with his sister. And since they would be working closely together from now on, who knew what might come of it? The Normans, for all their literary prominence, had never yet managed to marry into the aristocracy.

'Lord Rupert . . .' he began. The other man quickly waved a hand, sensing an ally in the ginger-haired drama critic. 'Please, call me Rupert,' he said. Then glanced once more at Alicia. 'Both of you must call me Rupert.'

'Thank you,' Neville beamed. 'Rupert. I believe our families are more or less neighbours? I must say, I've always admired Warrington Manor. It reminds me a little of Chatham.'

Rupert smiled. 'Thank you. We like it.' Rupert and Neville Norman gave each other a long, thoughtful look. A look of recognition. Of joined forces . . .

Alicia, trapped between them, felt herself struggling to breathe. Rupert Greyling-Simms was looking at her with such open admiration she knew she should be flattered. But she wasn't. For some reason, she felt scared. Which was ridiculous of course. What was there to be scared of?

Oh, if only Jared would look at her like that, as if she were an answer to his prayer.

Jared was looking at her, but he was also watching the mutual admiration society being forged between the two men. And he, too, felt a frisson of foreboding.

Neville Norman, however, was too happily contemplating what a perfect prospective countess his beautiful sister would make for Warrington Manor to think about anything else.

Rupert Greyling-Simms simply continued to stare intently at Alicia.

SIX

Gareth Lacey walked to the French windows that led into Hall and glanced inside. Long red velvet curtains hung at the windows and portraits lined the walls. His eyes, however, went straight towards High Table. Dinner seemed to be the only time he could nail her down nowadays. But that beautiful face with its wide green eyes was conspicuous by its absence.

He felt his heart sink. It was a full-fledged physical sensation, and he knew he should be alarmed at just how deeply involved with her he was becoming. But he couldn't bring himself to be sorry. He'd quickly found himself hooked, and he was glad. He would glance out of the window during the middle of a tutorial in the hopes of spotting the golden-haired siren, who seemed to want nothing to do with him. He found himself practically living in the SCR, just in the hopes that she might come in for a sherry and a blistering attack on Shakespeare's sonnets. She was not, he had discovered to everyone's horror, a Shakespeare fan.

When he thought of the intimate closeness of their first meeting, one part of him suspected her of blowing hot and cold in order to disorientate him. Of playing with him, like a cat played with a mouse. The thought made him feel giddy with desire. He was a man who had written books on the love affair between Lady Caroline Lamb and the 'mad, bad, and dangerous to know' Lord Byron. A man who admired a woman's femininity, her capriciousness, her claws, her passions, her cunning. A man who understood romance as a living, breathing, life-fulfilling concept. Being toyed with by Davina Granger was wonderful. It was bliss. It was making him feel alive, completely alive, for the first time in years. But another part of him wondered whether he'd totally misread the signs. Whether that spine-tingling conversation of theirs had been merely run-of-the-mill to her. It terrified him to think that she really might be as disinterested in him as she appeared. Having tasted the heady delights of being close to her, probing her delightfully convoluted psyche, bathing in the sights and sounds and scents of her, he wanted more. Much more.

He saw one or two of his students glance at him curiously and headed back for the stairs.

* * *

Davina paused outside Gareth's door and glanced around. With everyone in Hall, the silence was eerie. She knew she'd have to be quick and taking a deep breath she timidly knocked on the door, and then resolutely pushed it open. Nobody locked their doors in St Bede's, it seemed. As she switched on the light, she could see, to her relief, that the room was empty. Inside, with the door closed, her heart beat fast. Ridiculous to be so nervous, of course. She'd been at St Bede's long enough to have studied Gareth's every move.

She was just obviously not cut out to be a housebreaker.

Here, in his rooms, she could feel his presence all around her. Gareth. Just his name . . . Gareth . . . repeated in the quiet fortress of her mind could make every nerve ending in her body twitch. Finding herself enraptured by him so quickly, she'd been obliged to back off just a little, if only for her own peace of mind.

She needed to wean herself off that sensation of desire and intimacy whenever he was around. So far, unfortunately, it wasn't working. But he looked puzzled by her reticence, which was no good, of course. No good at all. She was going to have to bite the bullet sometime and make a much more positive move on him.

Not that that would be easy for her. Even in the staid and ultra-respectable SCR, his grey eyes had been capable of setting her skin jumping, her blood pounding, and her heart reluctantly racing. His lips were the most kissable she'd ever seen on a man.

Realising she was still standing with her back to the door, gazing around at the large, comfortably furnished den, she forced herself forward towards his desk with shaking knees. She sat down in a scuffed, faded red leather chair and felt herself sink into its contours. He'd sat in this chair for day after day, year after year, and he'd moulded it to his body. She could even smell him on the chair — the tangy scent of the pine aftershave he favoured. Grimly she fought off a sudden wave of intense desire. Yet she knew she would only have to close her eyes to conjure up his image in every sharp detail — those wings of brown hair over his forehead that always made her itch to run her fingers through them. Those eyes . . . She gave a small growl of real anger now and yanked open the first drawer of his desk.

Just get on with it, girl!

* * *

Gareth knocked on Davina's door in Wolsey. In his mind's eye he could see her opening it, her face bearing a fierce scowl, or that dreamy, otherworldly expression that meant that she'd been working on 'The Flame Moth'. She would laugh, ask him if that was the time already, and . . . But the door remained shut. He knocked again, his ears straining for the sound of movement within, but there was nothing.

Perhaps she was dining out of college tonight. The whole of Oxford knew that she was here by now. She was probably inundated with invitations. Grimly he walked back to the main door and stepped out on to the grass. Off to his right, the hoops of the croquet lawn glinted palely in the moonlight. It was a night for walking hand in hand along the banks of the Isis, watching the swans on the riverbank and listening to the choristers practising in Christ Church. The whole of Oxford was bathed in a full moon just waiting for him, and he had no Davina to share it with.

As he crossed the lawn towards Becket Arch, he glanced across at Walton. And saw that his lights were on.

* * *

Inside, Davina was feverishly flicking through the desk drawers. Her trawl so far wasn't very helpful — a student's essay he was in the middle of reading, a desk diary, assorted stationery. The next drawer down contained college printed papers, but the drawer under it, however, was locked. Her heart suddenly skipped a beat. A locked drawer usually meant something to hide.

Feverishly she tried the drawers on the left-hand side — all were open and one contained a small silver key, right at the back, hidden under a pile of brown envelopes. With a small whoop of triumph, she tried it in the locked drawer, mentally crossing her fingers as she turned the key. Yes! She pulled open the drawer and removed a large, heavy black folder. Heart beating, she opened it and began to read.

* * *

Outside, Gareth Lacey began to cross the lawn towards Walton. He was sure he'd turned off the light after dressing for dinner.

* * *

At first, Davina wasn't sure what it was that she was reading. It seemed to be a series of old exam papers, scribbled notes, research . . . Then she saw a letter from the principal of King Canute College in Banbury, and she suddenly realised what they were. Gareth was setting some exam papers for King Canute's summer exams. Damn!

She leaned back in the chair, feeling utterly dejected. But what had she expected? A secret diary, whereby he admitted bullying a student to the point of causing his suicide? A stack of ugly pornographic magazines? A . . . Suddenly she lurched upright on the chair and pulled the folder towards her again. Exam papers. Exam papers not yet finished, that students in King Canute would be sitting this summer . . .

She knew, of course, that Oxford dons were often asked to set papers for colleges outside Oxford, and that this was a very responsible job. Colleges had to ensure that nobody got to see them, save the department heads, before the exams were taken. No wonder he'd locked the drawer.

Davina began to feel dizzy with excitement. Here, at last, in these dry, cleverly designed questions, lay the key to Gareth Lacey's downfall. If only she could think how . . .

* * *

Gareth pushed open the heavy outer door to Walton and began to climb the set of stairs.

* * *

Davina leaned back in the chair, her mind racing. She could always photocopy a set of the questions when he'd finished them. But then what? And suddenly the idea popped into her head. Of course! If she could find a pupil at King Canute College willing to play along, she could give Gareth Lacey a taste of his own medicine, and then some!

See how he liked being branded a cheat.

All she had to do was bribe a pupil to say that he'd bought a set of the exam papers from Gareth Lacey! The money from her latest prize was still sitting in her bank account, doing nothing, so she could use some of that. She'd have to find a student who knew that he or she was likely to fail their English finals. Somebody who was lazy, who hadn't done the work . . . Just the sort of person who would buy exam papers in order to give him an edge. Just the sort of person, in fact, that a greedy examiner would try and sell them to.

Yes. Oh yes. David, oh, David, this revenge is going to be so sweet. So apt. So . . . poetic.

* * *

Outside, the thick carpet muffled the sounds of Gareth's footsteps as he walked along the corridor towards his door.

* * *

Quickly Davina gathered the folder together, carefully placed it in the drawer, relocked it, returned the key and got up out of the chair.

She walked to the door, looked around to make sure she'd left no sign of her presence, then turned off the light. A satisfied smile crossed her gamine face, and her green eyes glowed with satisfaction. At last! Step two could be put into operation. She opened the door and walked straight into Gareth Lacey's arms. The contact and the surprise and those damned stormy eyes of his knocked the breath right out of her. 'Gareth,' she said. 'I . . . was . . . looking for you.'

Gareth's hands had instinctively come out to catch her, and his surprise at having someone come out of his room instantaneously changed to an intense and sudden awareness that the whole wonderful length of her was pressed close against him. He dragged in a breath.

She heard it, and suddenly her own breathing fell to pieces.

Her knee was bent and pushing just between the gap in his legs. She was wearing a pair of worn jeans, with a white polo-neck jumper, and she could feel the warmth of his body penetrating the materials, making her own skin flush with borrowed, answering heat.

'Gareth,' she said again. He noticed her pupils dilate. Her lips fall open as she said his name. He knew he should do something. Say something. But he couldn't. At last, at *last*, what he'd wanted most in the world was suddenly his, and the only thing he could think to blurt out was something utterly banal and irrelevant.

'What were you doing in my room?' He didn't actually care what she'd been doing in his room. He only cared that she was now in his arms. Where he'd wanted her to be. Where he knew she had been destined to be. He believed that fate was a force of nature as tangible as any earth, wind or fire. From the moment he'd watched her walk towards him in the SCR in her lilac and silver dress, he'd known this moment was going to happen. Sometime. Somehow.

To Davina, however, his question sent every alarm bell ever invented clanging into her head. What could she tell him? To her own mind, her guilt must be written in huge red letters right across her forehead. In a flash, excuses flowed through her mind. I was leaving you a note . . . I thought you might like to walk me into Hall . . . I wanted your opinion about an anonymous poem I found in one of the books in the library . . .

None sounded feasible. All sounded pitiful. So she said the one thing she knew was guaranteed to distract him. And the one thing she'd wanted to say, above all other words, from the moment she'd first met him. 'I wanted to ask you to make love to me,' she said, her voice as soft as thistledown, her tone as demanding as nails.

Gareth felt the ground lurch beneath his feet. His arm around her waist tightened instinctively, as every inch of his body responded to her request. She watched the grey eyes churn into the dangerous waters of uncharted territory, and instead of feeling afraid — or even ashamed — she felt her stomach clench in a sudden, savage snap of sexual desire.

The hot moistness between her legs felt like fire. Her nipples, pressed against his dark blue jacket, suddenly stiffened with sensitivity, growing harder with every minute movement he made.

'But you weren't here,' she added, her voice a mere weak whisper now.

'I'm here now,' Gareth said gruffly. He began to move her backwards, into the darkened room, his heart pounding so hard it was like a drumbeat in his ears. After Martine, he'd never expected to find love again; and certainly never dreamed he'd find it in such an explosive, all-consuming way. What he felt for this woman was so urgent, so fierce and inescapable. It was as if she'd taken his safe and gentle life and shaken it as a dog shakes a rat.

Davina reached out to slam the door shut behind him. The moonlight shining through the window was their only illumination now, but it was enough. Her hands rose to curl around the lapels of his jacket. Such a formal garment. So right for dinner at High Table. She hated it! She attacked the buttons, then yanked it off his shoulders, letting it fall around their feet to be trampled and crushed. Underneath, the shirt he wore was white, cool-to-the-touch cotton, and she slowly lowered her head, letting her lips caress it, smelling once again that smell that was pure Gareth Lacey.

She kissed the cool soft material at his shoulder, feeling the warmth of his flesh beneath begin to penetrate. She dipped her head, using her now-sensitised lips to travel across the hard muscles of his chest.

Gareth groaned loudly, his voice echoing off the walls of his room.

In retaliation, Davina flicked out her tongue, moistening her lips, and then gently, tenderly, kissed the damp material, feeling his nipples harden beneath it. She pressed her hands hard into his shoulders and kissed him again lovingly.

Gareth threw his head back, the rich dark waves of his hair sliding back against his temples as his throat arched towards the ceiling. His mouth opened to let the sigh of pleasure escape. His legs threatened to buckle. He could feel a gathering tide of primitive passion rising up inside him. An undeniable, unconquerable sensation of desire that was about to drown him. He was eager to meet it. To swim in its currents. It had been so long since he'd felt so alive.

Davina closed her eyes as a swift, savage, bittersweet wave of loathing and longing surged through her. Without thinking about the folly of what she was doing, not caring a damn about the moral repercussions that tomorrow would bring, she reached out and ripped the shirt apart.

Pearl-white buttons snapped and zinged past her, one of them hitting a bare piece of floorboard at the edge of the rug with an audible 'ping'. Gareth's head snapped back upright. He looked down at the top of her head, the moonlight silvering the soft silky spikes of her hair as she slowly sank down to her knees in front of him. The sight of that nearly made him cry out again. Her fingers went to his zip, her palm slipping inside, the flat of her hand pressing hard against him.

Gareth moaned, a long, low, lingering sound that was wrenched out from the very depths of his masculinity. He felt himself harden further against her, pulsating into her palm, his very being straining for more and more of the intimate contact. He swayed towards her, so weak on his feet now, he wasn't sure he could stay standing. Davina loved the sound of his voice. Loved the way that sighing moan had sounded so . . . tortured. Good. She wanted to torture him. She wanted to make him groan and beg. She wanted to see that fine, handsome head of his thrashing from side to side as he fought back against the ecstasy. Wanted to . . .

Gareth reached down and lifted her from the floor. She gave a startled and surprised squeak, but the next instant found herself being laid across the desk. Snuff box, vase, papers and pens, all went slithering to the floor. She just had time to feel the ancient black leather of the centre of the desk pressing into her back, and then he was on top of her.

His dark hair fell across her forehead as he lowered his lips on to hers. Their mouths fused. She felt her lips tremble under the strength of his, felt his tongue remorselessly seek out hers. She felt the hard, pulsating length of him pressing insistently, urgently against her thigh. Felt her breasts compress against the solid wall of his chest. Her body melted with a honeyed, aching heat, and she kicked off her boots and reached down to her jeans, wriggling and arching her back as she tried to slide them down her trembling legs. He helped her, lifting her body, but never once taking his lips from hers.

They were breathing in each other's air now, exchanging the very stuff of life itself. He lifted his head at last to take in a fresh gulping breath, and then slid down the length of her, to pull the jeans free from her ankles.

She wasn't wearing any panties underneath.

The silver moonlight gilded the blonde triangle at the juncture of her thighs in a loving caress, casting deep and mysterious shadows across her skin. For a second or two he froze, stunned by the perfection of the sight. Then his hands moved up from her ankles, his questing fingers emerging on to the warm, trembling skin of her calves. His fingers gripped her legs with enough insistent pressure to pull them apart.

Davina felt her head fall back and dangle against the edge of the desk, giving her a kaleidoscopic upside-down view of the room. She felt his lips on her inner thigh and jerked spasmodically, her arms falling weakly by her side, her fingers curling around the edge of the wooden desk.

Gareth loved the smell of her, the hot, pulsating nearness of her very femininity. Gently, tentatively, probingly, he pressed his lips against her, kissing her, exploring her, breathing her in before finally delving his tongue deep into the very centre of her. This time Davina screamed. Her soft voice echoed clearly in the darkened, deserted building.

Her feet scrabbled and drummed helplessly against the ransacked drawers of the desk as her body convulsed and pulsated to his every flickering tongue-tip touch.

He cunningly discovered her engorged clitoris, and as she had sucked on his nipple, now he sucked on her, his hands coming out to press her waist firmly to the table as she tried to arch on the desk. His hands encountered the warm wool of her polo-neck jumper, and moved underneath it, reaching up, cupping her breasts. His thumbs found her nipples, and as he pressed his face harder against her, ruthlessly increasing the growing, spiralling pleasure there, so his thumbs stroked her breasts. Her body, explored on two pleasure fronts, quivered in satiated defeat.

Davina's head arched back in a spasm of ecstasy as her body shuddered in the dance of orgasm. She let out a long, wavering moan, then slowly collapsed back against the desk, weak and compliant in every pore.

Gareth looked up, a heady sense of accomplishment washing over him, then slowly moved back up her body, pulling the polo-neck up and over her head as he did so. Obediently she raised her arms, and he let the garment fall on to the floor beneath them. It glowed white in the moonlight against the dark rug. Gareth stared at her, hardly able to believe the beauty of her body. She was spread-eagled across the desk now, gloriously naked and silvered in the moonlight, her slim figure bathed in a fine sheen of perspiration that made her glow. She was breathing harshly — deep, ragged breaths that made her breasts rise and fall in agitation.

He groaned at the sight of those perfect, pale orbs, with their darkened cherry-coloured aureoles, and leaned forward to kiss them. Davina's hands came out to cup his dark head tenderly against her. His hair felt like pure silk beneath her fingertips. She pulled his head towards her, fastening her lips greedily on to his. It no longer mattered that he was also her enemy. It no longer mattered that she was intending to destroy him. Now, just at this moment, he was her lover, and she wanted him. She wanted his hard strength and powerful masculinity; to gain every last ounce of pleasure to be had for both of them before, totally exhausted, they sought oblivion in each other's arms.

Her hands went once more to his zip, and Gareth quickly knelt above her, his knees to either side of her waist as he helped her in her quest. Davina leaned forward to help as he quickly stripped the remaining clothes from his body, inflaming his ardour as she trailed her moist lips down the long line of his throat to the hollow at the base of his neck. Pressing featherlight kisses to the firm, tanned skin of his broad shoulders, she savoured the musky, masculine scent of his warm flesh, revelling in her power as his breathing became laboured, his tall frame shuddering in response to her increasingly intimate touch.

'I want you!' Davina pleaded, unable to bear the wait any longer. She clutched wildly at his shoulders, pulling him down on top of her and moaning helplessly as she wound her long legs about his strong torso, her whole being vibrating in response as he drove himself deeply into her. A low groan broke from his throat as he found himself encased in hot velvet, abandoning the struggle to maintain control as he surrendered to the sweetest temptation of all.

It had been a long time since he'd made love to a woman, let alone a firebrand like Davina, but he instinctively knew that this encounter would be like no other. And Davina also found herself transported to another plane, transfixed with wonder and unable to believe that what had initially started out as part of her revenge had now led to her being helplessly caught in the overwhelmingly erotic toils of her own over-whelming need and desire.

The shafts of pale moonlight were throwing into sharp relief the chiselled planes of his face — the clenched jaw, the expanse of his high cheekbones, the contours of his firm mouth. He looked magnificent, an almost primeval male animal who was filling her with his strong hard length.

'Open your eyes . . . look at me,' she begged, needing to glimpse those grey eyes darken in helpless desire, to see them widening in ecstasy as he reached his climax. Whatever her original plan, she now desperately wanted . . . helplessly needed . . . the satisfaction which it seemed that only *this* man could give her.

When his eyes snapped open there was fire in those storm-grey depths. A slight smile played on his lips as he gazed down at her tenderly. And then, firmly in the grip of his passionate need, his eyes grew cloudy and opaque as the slow rhythmic movements of his body gave way to increasingly more powerful thrusts as he lunged into her, again and again.

Her body writhed helplessly beneath him, but there was no escape from the pleasure-giving power of his love-making. Gareth watched as the tight, tension-filled expression on her face gradually altered, giving way to a dazed smile of sheer, exquisite ecstasy, and then became aware of his own body responding to her helpless moans; the sound igniting a flame of red-hot passion, burning with a scorching, ever-increasing intensity and now totally beyond his control.

'Davina!' he whispered. 'My wonderful, wicked, dangerous . . . *Davina*!'

She cried out and arched as the world around her seemed to shatter into fragments of light and power. She lost all conscious thought as her whole frame was convulsed by an orgasm so powerful that it seemed as though she was going to faint. Her mind went to a place it had never been before. Her body fused with his, seemed to merge and then re-emerge, changed for ever. Gareth felt himself explode into her. Felt the strength leave his arms as he collapsed on top of her. He didn't know whether he was alive or dead. He didn't care. He only knew he never wanted to feel any other way, for as long as he lived.

SEVEN

March had come in, not like a lion but like a sunburst, determined to spread goodwill and the joys of spring. In his room, Jared rolled out of bed and pushed open his creaky, diamond lead-paned window. The daffodils were blooming in golden ranks outside the library, and a blackbird was singing to his mate in the ancient, twisted ivy.

It was a perfect day for punting on the Cherwell. Being midweek, and March, he doubted it would be overrun. He had, of course, no intention of messing about on the water on his own. Oh no. He had a definite companion in mind.

He dressed carefully in his new shirt and began to whistle. He reached for his best pair of jeans, pulled on socks, then trainers. A thorough brushing of his teeth, a very quick brush of his tangled mop of hair, and he was ready. He didn't, however, head straight for Webster. Instead he went out of one of the postern gates, moving into a full-fledged loping run as he headed towards Little Clarendon Street. There he found the small, select, rather pricey shop that served as a second pantry to the more well-heeled members of the Oxford colleges.

He knew it was madness to splurge so much on a picnic, but what the hell? If March could rouse itself to present him with such a warm morning, he could go wild too. Besides, working as a waiter in Browns during the holidays was no great hardship. If he bankrupted himself this morning, he had all of the Easter vacation to earn some more cash.

The moment he stepped into the small, dark, higgledy-piggledy shop, the plethora of stomach-rumbling smells hit him. Freshly baked garlic bread, meats and cheeses, and the more exotic offerings of oysters and Parma ham.

He picked up a wicker basket and began to make careful choices, selecting two ripe peaches, a soft, creamy Brie, a loaf of still-hot French bread and a farmhouse pâté. Deciding he might as well be in for a penny as for a pound, he added a half-bottle of champagne and two cartons of orange juice to make some Buck's Fizz.

He paid for his choices at the counter, emptying his pockets with determined cheerfulness. If life wasn't for the living, then what was it for? He left the shop, wishing he had a proper picnic basket, and as he jogged back to college, Jared suddenly remembered whom he could scrounge one from.

* * *

Alicia was at her desk, planning out the essay Dr Lacey had set her yesterday. She rather thought that he suspected her secret ambition to write murder mysteries, for he'd given her a piece on Edgar Allan Poe's 'Murders in the Rue Morgue'. Of course, he'd asked her to compare the style of that short story to his poem 'The Raven', but even so . . .

The sudden rap on the door was so loud in the quiet building that it made her nearly jump out of her skin. When she threw open the door to see Jared standing there, a wide grin on his face and an intriguing wicker picnic hamper in his hand, she felt the familiar sense of flustered excitement warm her face.

'Jared. I didn't think we were meeting until tonight,' she said, returning his smile. They were due to have another play-plotting blitz after dinner.

'True. But have you seen the day outside?'

Alicia had. Such brilliant sunshine was hard to miss.

She glanced down at the hamper, trying not to get her hopes up.

'I can see you're studying,' Jared said softly, glancing at the chaos on her desk, 'but I was hoping to lure you out on to the Cherwell. For a punt, a picnic . . . perhaps a song or two, if we stop off at Christ Church to listen to the choirboys practise . . .'

Alicia caught her breath. It sounded so ideal. So romantic. 'With me?' she asked stupidly. Jared looked into those wide, surprised blue eyes, and laughed. 'No, with your friend Emily. Of course with you, twit!'

Alicia blushed. 'Oh.'

Jared waited, then swapped the picnic basket to his other hand. 'I would like an answer before the end of term, if you don't mind,' he teased outrageously. She was so easy to tease, it was almost irresistible.

Alicia flushed again. 'Oh. Yes. Of course. I . . . er . . . I'll get my coat.' He watched her snatch up a grey raincoat. She was wearing a pale lavender cashmere sweater over cream linen trousers. Her long mass of raven-black hair was caught up in a mauve and cream silk scarf, the ends of which hung down her back among the raven tresses. She looked ready for the catwalk, let alone a slightly dusty, slightly damp punt. She tossed the grey coat around her shoulders and gave him a brilliant smile.

Jared tried to catch his breath, thought better of it, and shrugged ruefully instead. When he was around Alicia, he was getting used to experiencing breathing difficulties. He held the door wide open for her, and with an exaggerated arm gesture and bend of the waist, he bowed her through the door. 'Shall we go?'

They walked slowly down St Giles, up to Carfax, where the mechanical figures came out to chime the hour of ten o'clock. Then up the High Street, past Lincoln College, All Souls, Queen's, and St Edmund Hall, past the aptly named Long Wall Street and finally towards Magdalen Bridge and the small punt rental shack not far from Magdalen College itself.

Jared selected the best, newest (and driest) punt, and reached for a long fibre-glass pole, getting in with ease. Alicia, amused and awed by his casual demeanour, allowed herself to be guided gallantly into the punt, and sat, a bit gingerly, on the middle strut.

'No, no, not like that,' Jared said, sorrowfully shaking his head. 'You're supposed to lean back at the far end and drape your arm gracefully over the side to trail a few maidenly fingers into the water.'

Alicia grinned, and obligingly sat at the far end, stretching out in a surprisingly comfortable position on the floor of the punt. But her fingers she was keeping strictly to herself. Warm day or not, it was still March, and she was not about to stick her hand into an icy river!

It had been some time since Jared had last been in a punt. After a few false starts, some hilarious wobbles and frantic windmilling of arms, he finally managed to push away from the jetty, pole them out into the middle of the river and to manoeuvre them, with growing skill and confidence, under Magdalen Street and away from the sound of the city's traffic. The simple action of pole in, firm push, pole out, quick but smooth hand action back to the top of the pole for the next push, soon came back to him.

They hadn't rushed their walk up the High Street, so it was already past eleven o'clock when they encountered the loop in the river just past the bridge, and he poled the punt towards the right, where St Hilda's sprawled.

Almond blossom was out everywhere, lacing the river-banks, roads and gardens with frothing pink blossom. The sun was so high now, and so unseasonably warm, that Alicia slipped the grey coat from her shoulders and leaned her head back, tilting her face up to the sun. Jared, watching her, very nearly lost his pole. He hastily freed it, brought it smoothly back up, and ruefully told himself to concentrate on his river craft, unless he wanted to find them floating helplessly in the current without any way of making it to the nearest bank!

In front and slightly to the left of them loomed the vast green expanse of Christ Church Meadow with its browsing cattle, a pastoral delight right in the heart of the city.

'I thought this Oxford only existed in Evelyn Waugh novels,' Alicia murmured, thinking of *Brideshead Revisited*. 'I can't believe it's only March. It feels like high summer.'

'I know,' Jared murmured, keeping a wary eye on a pair of nesting swans on the far bank. Alicia saw them too and sat up. 'Oh, Jared look! Aren't they lovely? Have we got any bread for them?'

'We have. Some very prestigious, freshly baked French bread. But I don't think it's a good idea.'

'Skinflint!' she teased, flashing him a white-toothed grin.

'Miserliness has nothing to do with it!' he defended himself righteously. 'If you weren't such a city slicker, you'd know that they're nesting and breeding right now, and the cob can get very territorial. The last thing we want is for him to think we're making improper advances to his mate and come flapping over here, honking and hissing, and capsizing us!'

'Chicken!' she jeered, then wondered at her own bravery. She'd never teased and bantered with a man like this before. Would never even have considered it.

Jared grunted. 'Hah! You say that now, but if he started coming over here, flapping those enormous wings of his, you'd soon start singing a different tune!'

Alicia thought he was probably right.

The weeping willows were almost yellow, as their tightly furled buds began to uncurl. A soft bellowing from one of the cows in the meadows echoed peacefully across the river. It was hard to believe there was traffic, and a thriving modern city, going about its business all around them.

St Hilda's came and went on their right, and Jared, spotting a bend in the river, nestling among a stand of weeping willows, instinctively steered the punt towards it.

Because she was travelling with her back to where they were going, the first Alicia knew of his proposed landing place was when a strand of leafy weeping willow brushed past her cheek. She caught it then let it trail out of her hand, entranced. Soon they were nudging their way through a whole curtain of weeping willow branches to the steep green bank beyond. The punt nudged into the bank, coming to rest with a gentle bump. Jared poled them into a parallel position to the bank, then looped the mooring rope into the air, over one of the thicker branches, and tied it off.

With the high bank on one side, and the screen of trailing, weeping willow branches on the other, they found themselves cocooned in their own secret green world. 'It's like a fairy tale,' Alicia breathed, as a Jenny Wren suddenly trilled from the gnarled roots of a nearby willow.

'I know,' Jared said, overawed as much as she. He'd wanted to spend the day with her, away from college and their friends and work and the play. He'd wanted to make it romantic, and peaceful and special. But not even he could have hoped for something as perfect as this. He carefully laid the pole inside the punt, then reached for the picnic hamper. He moved towards her, the punt rocking gently with his surefooted movements, and sat down on the middle strut, the picnic hamper between them. The noon sun, beating down through the canopy of willow, cast dappled light across her. One diamond of sunlight was lying across her left eye, turning the china blue into a brilliant Ceylon sapphire.

She blinked lazily.

'You look beautiful,' Jared said hoarsely.

Alicia blinked again, this time feeling anything but lazy. 'I do?' she blurted.

Jared nodded, then quickly ducked his head to unfasten the hamper. He felt suddenly nervous. Shy, almost.

Alicia stared at the bent head, a warm rush of tenderness flooding over her. Underneath all that banter and laughter he was as nervous and unsure of himself as she was.

'Let's see — we have pâté, with fresh crusty bread. A knife.'

'Thank you.'

'We have Brie . . . hope you like Brie.'

'I love Brie.'

'Peaches.'

'I love peaches.'

'And . . . ta-dah!' he held up a battered blue thermos.

'Coffee?' Alicia hazarded blankly.

'Coffee?' Jared growled, looking scandalised. 'I'll have you know, peasant, that while you were tucked up in bed, snoring happily away, I was slaving over a hot blender, just to make you some Buck's Fizz.'

'I don't snore!'

Jared reached into the picnic hamper and extracted a pair of cut crystal glasses. He'd borrowed them from the same chap who had the hamper, under dire threats of disembowelment if he should break either of them. Now he placed the sparkling Waterford crystal flutes on the floor of the punt and carefully poured out the sparkling champagne and orange juice from the flask. Solemnly he handed a glass to her.

'To you,' he said softly. Alicia felt her hand shaking slightly as she accepted the glass from him.

'To the director,' she whispered. They clinked glasses even more solemnly and drank. It was perfect — the champagne was dry, but the orange juice was sweet. 'Mmm . . . wonderful.'

Jared busied himself with breaking the bread into chunks and layering on the pâté. Alicia watched him, wanting to say something, something that would honour this wonderful day and this wonderful setting, but she couldn't think what.

She wanted to blurt out 'I love you' but of course she didn't. She might not know much about men, but even she knew that saying something like that was bound to scare a bloke out of his wits. But she rather thought . . . she rather feared . . . that she did love him.

Jared looked up, caught that look, and froze.

For a second he couldn't believe what he was seeing. He'd been dreaming of seeing just that look in those stunning blue eyes ever since the first day Emily had introduced them. Slowly, cautiously, he leaned forward, as if expecting any moment to see her jump up and run away. But as he leaned over her, carefully placing his knees either side of her on the flat bottom of the punt, she began to lean towards him, not away. Her lips fell slightly open. He could hear her take in a sudden, deep breath. The air around them seemed to quiver, sigh, and then still into utter tranquillity as his lips dipped towards her. His hand came up to cup her cheek, and discovered that her skin was so soft against his fingers that it felt like padded satin.

He caught a waft of the scent from her hair — fresh violets.

She swayed further towards him. Her heartbeat suspended. When their lips finally met, he felt a jolt go through him, as if he'd been hit by an invisible bolt of lightning.

She tasted sweet, of champagne and oranges and something more . . . something so utterly feminine, so totally Alicia, that he had to hold himself back from dragging her into his arms and trying to absorb the very essence of her.

Alicia's eyes feathered closed, the image of his melting-chocolate eyes and waves of nut-brown hair remaining imprinted on the back of her retinas. With her eyes closed, she was in a world of sound, smell, taste and darkness. She could feel the cold and warm patches on her hands and face, where sunlight and shadow took it in turns to caress her. She could feel his fingers on her cheek, four tiny points of heat radiating through her, and the heat from his thumb under her chin. She could smell him — the scent of soap and aftershave, new shirt and man.

The water lapped at the punt, causing the tiniest waves of movement beneath them. She felt, quite literally, as if she were floating . . . And, over and above all of that, superseding everything, the touch of his lips on hers. Cool but warm. Firm but gentle. Simple, but meaning everything. A kiss that seemed to go on for ever.

Her own hand came out to cup his head, her fingers smoothing a path through the thick mass of cool hair to the warm scalp beneath. She opened her mouth wider, inviting deeper, greater intimacies. Jared groaned. It was such a sudden, unexpected, primitive sound that it startled her.

Jared felt her instinctive surprised withdrawal immediately. And, before Alicia could stop him, he lifted his lips, leaning back, hoping he didn't look as completely shattered as he felt. He'd kissed women before. Had done more, much more than that. But nothing had prepared him for the perfection of such a moment; a moment that now was gone for ever. It left a bittersweet taste in his soul.

Alicia sighed. She wanted him back where he'd been. Wanted to tell him that she'd been caught unawares, that was all, and that she wasn't scared, wasn't . . .

But he was already leaning back on his heels, his hands falling away from her face. And although she loved his smile, she hated the smile he gave her now, because it meant he was moving further away from her. Dragging them back to that other place called reality.

As if to prove her right, Jared, telling himself it would be a disaster to rush her, struggled for something to say, and managed to shrug one shoulder nonchalantly.

'We'd better finish the Buck's Fizz before it gets warm.'

A drake mallard, discovering their hideaway, swam beneath the canopy of willow and quacked hopefully for a piece of the feast. The comical sound finally snapped Alicia out of her dreamlike trance. She looked at the duck, at his glossy emerald head and curly tail, and smiled tremulously. 'I don't think this chap is in danger of sinking us,' she laughed determinedly, and tossed him a piece of bread, fiercely telling herself that she could be as adult about all this as Jared.

She must get rid of this stupid idea that a single kiss meant something. In this day and age, it really meant nothing. Nothing at all. Jared must have kissed a lot of girls, and probably didn't even remember their names now.

She thought about Emily, who changed her boyfriends as casually as her father changed his socks, and sternly told herself to pull herself together. She accepted a plate of crusty bread and pâté and ate it, and then talked about the play and fed the duck, trying to cover up her discomfort.

Jared, fighting off an almost overwhelming urge to rush across the punt and ravish her, told himself to be satisfied with his progress. After today, she couldn't possibly see him as just the director of the play, one of the lads, a mere friend. After this magical picnic, that earth-shattering kiss, she must know that she was very special to him . . .

The most special thing in the world, in fact.

* * *

Davina raised an eyebrow as Gareth led her through the dark and deserted car park towards a white Jaguar XJS. Dinner was long over, and when he'd invited her to go with him to a local nightclub that had a jazz evening every Tuesday, she'd quickly accepted.

'I wouldn't have guessed you were a sports car driver,' she said over the roof of the low-slung car, as he delved into his pocket for the keys. 'I have an E-type myself.'

Gareth looked at her over the expanse of white roof, thinking about that classic, curvaceous, serious car. 'Yes,' he said simply. 'It suits you.'

Davina felt again that pang of connection, that sensation of souls meeting. Damn him, what right did he have to know how she felt about her car? He opened the passenger door and she slid in angrily, dropping her scuffed leather handbag at her feet as Gareth unlocked his own door and climbed in behind the wheel. Ever since they'd made love on the desk, she'd found it impossible to get him out of her mind.

A week spent working furiously on the anthology hadn't helped distract her. Nor had hiring a private detective to find a pupil at the King Canute College to fit her bill.

She knew that he was taking it for granted that they were 'an item' now. As was the rest of the college. Nobody, from disgruntled female students to highly interested dons, had failed to note their intense closeness. And as he drove them towards Holywell, and a small, smoky club that had the meanest sax player Davina had ever heard, she knew that that suited her just fine. She'd spun her web and caught her fly.

But soon, now, he was going to want a repeat performance of that mind-blowing evening on his desk. And she was going to have to make up her mind whether or not she could afford to go through with it again. Already her body was beginning to feel more his than hers. As he slipped off her coat in the tiny cramped cloakroom and led her on to the packed dance floor, she could feel herself melt against him, no matter what furious directions to the contrary her mind gave to her wayward flesh and blood. Her arms felt languorous as they slipped over his shoulders. Her hips, moving against his as they swayed to the slow, blues beat of the music, seemed boneless. The pale red and blue lights gleamed on the dark wings of his hair, reflected in the grey of his eyes. He kissed her hard, moulding her lips to his, his mouth insistent and hungry on hers.

She kissed him back, as hard, as angry, as hungry. But then, deliberately, determinedly, she drew back from him. More out of a desire to prove to herself that she could than as a punishment for him.

'Let's find a table and a drink,' she murmured, annoyed to find her voice coming out so huskily.

They found a tiny round table over by the back door. A cold draught was blowing through from under it, as the night outside turned progressively more frosty.

'What do you want?' Gareth asked, and for a moment she felt like laughing. What did she want? Then she reminded herself that all she wanted was revenge for David. And to see this man broken. This man who could set her blood burning with just a look. This man who could touch her soul with his understanding of her poetry.

'Vodka. Neat,' she said tensely.

He nodded and fought his way to the bar. By the time he came back, Davina was in no mood to be merciful.

'Well, I've made twenty choices for the anthology so far,' she said briskly, accepting the drink and taking a good gulp without so much as a wince. 'But I don't know how strong my conviction is going to be when I've picked out a hundred and twenty and some poems have to go.'

Gareth nodded. 'I don't envy you. It's at times like these that I'm glad I'm just a simple teacher.'

Davina smiled grimly. How modest. 'But even teaching is not always plain sailing is it?' she said in a dulcet tone, by not a flicker of an eyelash giving him warning of what was to come. 'I heard from Rex this morning that you lost one of your pupils last term. A boy, he said. He implied a great tragedy.'

It was difficult to tell in the dim light, but she was sure that he suddenly paled. 'What happened?' she pressed. She suddenly wanted, more than anything, to hear his pathetic excuses. But Gareth shook his head.

'I don't talk about it,' he said flatly.

Davina felt a wave of screaming rage swamp her. For one insane moment she wanted to reach across the table and attack him, beating him with her fists, telling him that her brother was more important than that. That he should talk about nothing else but that gentle, funny, wonderful boy who'd wanted to teach as well. And who now lay in his grave.

'I see,' she said. 'Sorry that I'm not worthy to be trusted with your secrets,' she flashed, and got to her feet.

Gareth opened his mouth, then firmly closed it again. If Davina was in no mood to be merciful, he was in no mood to respond to emotional blackmail.

They were silent as they drove back to college. Silent as he walked her to the door of Wolsey. Silent as she walked to her own door within the building and opened it. When she turned, he already knew she was not going to invite him in. He was becoming adept at reading her mercurial moods.

Instead of exasperating him, they satisfied him. She had the soul of a poet after all — she was a woman unlike any other; she was entitled to be capricious. Having given him a taste of heaven, she was now determined to starve him.

Well, that was all right with him too.

For a while, anyway.

When she turned, her lips already opening to give him words of dismissal, he reached for her, dragging her into his arms. She struggled wildly for the briefest of seconds, but then his lips were on hers, and all the fight went out of her. His arms around her waist felt like wonderful chains.

The kiss was hard, angry, brief, but satisfied something in both their psyches. When he pulled back and looked down into glowing green eyes, flashing viciousness and desire in equal measures, he slowly nodded.

'I'm not giving up on you, Davina,' he said softly. 'Try as hard as you like, I'm not going to let you chase me away.'

A strange, almost feral look crossed her face. A look that was not frightened, not challenging, not disbelieving, but somehow . . . ironically amused . . .

'Good,' Davina said softly. 'Because I have plans for you, too.'

EIGHT

Jared reached for Alicia's hand and squeezed it reassuringly. 'Relax — it'll be fine.' They were sitting in the front row of the theatre, and the cast were about to do their first run-through of the complete play.

She wished she had Jared's laid-back attitude. She wished . . . She wished Jared would kiss her, as he had on the punt.

The door at the back opened, and Davina Granger approached them. 'Hello, I heard there was a rehearsal going on.'

'That's right. I'm Jared Cowan, the director. You're welcome to watch, but I warn you, there'll be plenty of mistakes to be ironed out.'

Although he was speaking to Davina, he was talking more for Alicia's benefit. He wanted her to be prepared for the chaos that the first run-through always produced.

Davina laughed. 'Ah, but that's where all the fun's to be had,' she pointed out.

Jared believed her. 'Miss Granger, I'd like to introduce you to the author of the play, Alicia Norman . . .'

Behind him, Alicia went hot then cold. As he turned, and Davina glanced across him towards her, she quickly rose from the chair, spilling her script, notes and pen around her.

Confused, she made a made a mad dip to pick them up, then thought how silly she must look and stood upright again, then didn't know what to do with her hands and stuck them behind her back, then thought how silly that must look and let them drop to her sides. Finally she managed what felt to her like an inane grin.

Davina watched this shy, awkward, endearingly touching scene, and suddenly St Agnes snapped into her mind. This woman was so childlike. And those huge blue eyes . . . all that medieval long dark hair . . . 'Hello,' Davina said, reaching forward to shake the woman's hand. 'It takes courage to take on a big project like this. I admire your nerve.'

Alicia took the hand nervously. According to her aunt, Davina was pioneering the art of twenty-first-century poetry for women almost single-handedly.

'She's written a wonderful play,' Jared said staunchly, and Davina smiled. It was not hard to interpret the look in the wide blue eyes of her St Agnes. Young love. There was nothing quite like it.

Behind them the door opened once again, and Davina recognised Neville Norman. 'Miss Granger,' he gushed, 'I was hoping to run into you again. Alicia,' Neville turned to his sister. 'How's the play coming?' he asked politely.

Alicia wished she knew.

'We're about to have our first run-through,' Jared said. 'I'm sure you know what they're like. If you'd like to meet up with us later . . .'

Neville smiled. 'Oh, but I love watching the bare bones of a play being padded out,' he contradicted, and very deliberately moved to one of the front-row seats. Davina tried not to smile as Jared glowered at his elegant back. Then the smile faded as she noticed the agonised look on the beautiful face of her St Agnes. Of course, she thought, as she made the connection. Neville Norman was the big brother and famous theatre critic, here to watch her play. No wonder the poor girl looked as if she'd rather be somewhere else. Anywhere else . . . like on the bridge of the *Titanic* for instance.

Instantly, Davina began to cast Neville as the villain of her poem. She could use his sartorial elegance like a battering ram. Lampoon the man's obvious ego, turn him into the voracious monster who would bring doom to her luckless heroine . . .

'Places then,' Jared called out reluctantly as Davina took a seat next to Alicia. 'Let's have a run-through — no interruptions,' Jared carried on. 'I'll be timing the changes.' He moved to the front row, placing himself between Neville and his sister. If the creep wanted to start sneering, he'd have to get through Jared first.

'Right. Act One, Scene One. When you're ready . . .' And so it began, the first ever run-through of *The Estate of Matrimony*.

Alicia made copious notes. As the rehearsal drew to an end, Jared slumped down next to Alicia and sighed.

'That was fascinating,' Davina was the first to break the silence. 'You thought of the whole plot?' she asked Alicia.

'Oh, Jared and Emily helped.' She indicated the ginger-haired girl on the stage. 'But it needs work.'

Davina smiled. 'All first drafts do. Isn't that right, Neville?' she added, silkily using the man's first name in order to put him on the spot. Jared, very discreetly, hid a grin behind his hand while Neville rose to the occasion magnificently.

'Of course. The play has a lot of merit. But that appalling bit of sloppy work in Act Two, Scenes Four and Five, needs major repairs.'

'I've already got notes and thoughts on that,' Alicia said, with just a hint of bite to her voice, missing the stunned look that Neville gave her. It was the first time in his life he could remember his sweet and compliant sister answering him back in that way.

Davina and Jared both felt like applauding.

'I think you'll come up with something really special, Alicia,' Rupert Greyling-Simms, who'd been waiting for his chance, chose that moment to step into the fray. Jared's head snapped up as Rupert approached. Davina, who knew nothing about the background of the leading man, looked at him thoughtfully. As far as outward appearances were concerned, he was a veritable blond Adonis.

'Thanks for the vote of confidence,' Alicia laughed shakily. 'I hope I don't let you down,' she raised her voice to include the rest of the cast but nobody believed that she would. They could all tell that it was basically a good play.

'You won't,' Rupert said firmly. 'Now, I've ordered some smoked salmon and champagne to be delivered to Jared's room,' he called over to the stage. 'Hope everyone has an appetite.'

The cast began to applaud and catcall, while Jared thought of the beer and crisps he'd organized and grimaced wryly.

'Right,' Jared called out loudly. 'Meet here again tomorrow for script changes.' There were groans and good-natured mutters, and a general exodus towards Jared's room in Wolsey.

'Well, the library awaits me,' Davina murmured. 'Alicia, I liked the play a lot. Have you ever thought of writing a whodunit? I think you could give Ruth Rendell et al. a real run for their money.'

Alicia's blue eyes widened like those of an owl. 'Really? Do you really think so?'

'I doubt my sister would want to do anything so run-of-the-mill, Miss Granger,' Neville stepped in smoothly.

Jared opened his mouth to tell the idiot to shut up, but Davina got there ahead of him. 'Oh? You think that genre is run-of-the-mill? I'm surprised,' she purred. 'I've always found that particular area very rich in talent. In my opinion, Margery Allingham's "Campion" is a fine creation. Every bit as good as Dorothy L. Sayers' "Lord Peter Wimsey".'

Neville forced a smile on to his lips. 'Of course. The twenties and thirties were a classic era for whodunits. But nowadays . . .' he spread his hands in a dismissive gesture.

Rupert shifted restlessly, impatient to have Alicia to himself. During the last few weeks, he felt that they had established a real rapport. Although she didn't pick him out for special attention, Rupert knew that that was just a cover. She was so shy; she didn't want to make her attraction for him obvious. But he was getting weary of pretending they were just friends. It was time to make his move. She was so beautiful. So alive. He must hear her say those magic words to him, soon. Say to him, 'I love you.' Rupert reached out and took Alicia by the arm. She was so surprised — she'd actually forgotten he was still there — that she felt herself moving forward. 'Why don't we leave them to argue,' he said softly, 'while we go and drink champagne?'

Jared went white at this openly aggressive move. He made an instinctive gesture towards them as Rupert began to lead Alicia away, but Neville quickly blocked him. 'Not so fast, Cowan! I don't want you encouraging Alicia in this damned silly fantasy of hers . . .'

Davina saw that Jared was more than capable of dealing with the Neville Normans of this world, and with a discreet excuse, moved away. It had been a real breather to get away from the enigmatic and painful puzzle that was Gareth Lacey for a short while. But now his spectre was back. As Davina headed towards the library, her shoulders uncharacteristically slumped, Alicia found herself being escorted to Jared's room not by Jared, but by Rupert Greyling-Simms.

'I think you've been very clever,' he said admiringly. 'And my character is very complex, isn't he?'

'Yes, and you play him so well,' she assured him hastily. What were Jared and her brother talking about back there?

'Thank you,' Rupert said, his face glowing at her praise.

'I can really sympathise with him. He loves Susan so much,' he carried on, his eyes feasting hungrily on her face. 'She's his whole world. He simply has to have her all to himself. He can't bear to share her with her husband and children.'

He thought of his father, back at Warrington Manor, and his heart lurched. He was a brute of a man, who lived merely to hunt and fish on his estates and mock his only son. According to his father, Rupert was a failure, a dead loss, a miserable wretched excuse for a son and heir. He thought of his mother, a voracious spender of money and excruciating social snob, and of his sister. Daddy's precious pet. His biggest rival . . .

But when he returned home with this prize — Alicia Norman — then his family would see. His father, with his expert eye for women, would love her. Even he would have to admit that his son had chosen a beauty. His snobbish mother would be forced to admit that a Norman was a class act, for Alicia's father was to be mentioned in the next New Year's Honours List, if the current rumours were to be believed. And as for his sister . . . well, Alicia would put paid to his father's threats to leave the family fortune to her! As soon as he produced a grandson for the old man, Rupert knew his fortune would be secured. And this gorgeous, enchanting, precious creature beside him was just the woman to turn his life around. Secure a happy future. Provide him with the love that no one else had ever chosen to give him.

'Tell me, Alicia, have you ever seen Warrington Manor . . . ?' he murmured.

They climbed the stairs to Wolsey together, Alicia's mind on Jared. But when Jared strolled in a few minutes later, it was to find Alicia and Rupert over in one corner, talking animatedly, and Jared cast them a thoughtful, worried look. There was something odd about Rupert. He'd noticed it quite a few times recently — especially when he was playing the part of Sam Blake, the killer. His performance of teetering on the edge of insanity was just a shade too convincing. And Jared wondered, uneasily, about the nature of the man's obvious infatuation with Alicia. It wasn't . . . normal. Oh, he knew that a woman as beautiful as Alicia was bound to attract men like moths to a flame, and he was more than prepared to fight them off. But Rupert . . . There was something . . . *pathetic* about Rupert that worried him. Made him unsure how to proceed. He also knew that Alicia was hardly aware of Rupert's existence, and she was so damned green when it came to men that she was probably missing all the signals . . .

Neville didn't miss the thoughtful and worried look on Jared's face, and frowned. Neville was nobody's fool; he could see that Jared was falling for his sister, and Alicia, the silly chump, was just the sort of romantic fool who might just be persuaded to go for a penniless engineer rather than a rich Lord of the Realm.

He had to think of a way to break them up . . .

He wandered aimlessly around Jared's room, chatting to the crush of people inside, and then, on a desk strewn with engineering books, noticed Jared's cheque book, lying out in plain sight, and that gave Neville a brilliant idea. Glancing casually around, making sure that no one was looking, he made a quick note of Jared's account number, then went downstairs to the public telephone in the hall to put through a call to his bank.

He wanted to transfer five . . . no, ten thousand pounds into Jared Cowan's account. A payoff to leave his sister alone. Of course, Jared knew nothing about it. But Alicia wouldn't know that. And wouldn't believe that, either, when he told her that her precious Jared had been bought off.

NINE

Davina stepped off the train at Banbury Station and hailed a taxi. She knew her heart wasn't in what she was doing, and she growled warnings to herself as she got into the back of the cab, like a she-wolf with a recalcitrant bone.

'King Canute College, please,' she said crisply. It was her head that was ruling this show. That settled, she looked around her, leaning forward as they neared the famous cross. The words of the nursery rhyme flickered across her mind.

Ride a cock horse to Banbury Cross,
To see a fine lady upon a white horse,
With rings on her fingers and bells on her toes,
She shall have music wherever she goes.

But no poem echoed back at her. Nothing was coming to her today, except a vague but persistent depression. It was that damned man's fault. Gareth Lacey. He'd come into her life like one of the plagues of Egypt, utterly destroying everything good. David — dead. Her own peace of mind — gone. Her life upside down. Her body no longer her own. Just thinking about him set up a familiar sweet ache deep in her abdomen. She could feel her skin tingle in anticipation of his touch. Already she could hear his voice in her mind, talking about all the things that were important to her: life, poetry, experience, love, humanity . . .

Damn it! Concentrate on the matter in hand, she snarled at herself angrily. And it was good advice, for the taxi had arrived.

There was not a soul about. Obviously, everyone was in class. By following battered signs with missing letters, she eventually found her way to the administration building. There, the principal's secretary, who was expecting her, gave a discreet buzz on the intercom, and the inner door promptly opened, revealing a beaming bald man who swept forward.

'Miss Granger, I can't tell you how pleased I am to meet you,' he gushed, thrusting out his hand.

Davina took it and felt a sudden shaming rush of guilt. This man's honesty was written across his face for all to see, and she felt, suddenly, dirty and shabby in comparison.

'Hello, Mr Morgan.' She smiled as best she could. 'Thank you for agreeing to see me at such short notice.'

She'd written to him only three days ago, requesting a meeting, hinting at her availability to give a lecture to the college's English students.

'That's no problem at all,' he assured her, ushering her into his office. There was a threadbare carpet, battered desk and wilting greenery, but somehow the energetic presence of the principal seemed to override it.

Davina felt like a Judas, here to bring shame and disgrace on them. For when the news hit that Gareth Lacey had been caught selling exam papers to a student at this college, would Mr Morgan be beaming so happily? She somehow doubted it. But, as if to rebut that, flashing into her mind came a sudden stark vision of David's funeral.

It had been a raw December day, wet and bleak as they'd watched the coffin being lowered into a cold, dark grave. It had been almost impossible to believe that under the white lilies was the fun-loving, generous-hearted boy she'd adored.

To Davina he'd always been someone to love and protect.

After she'd left school and begun her wanderlust days, they'd sent each other long chatty letters. She could almost picture his beloved St Bede's from his description of it. And then, after just a year, his letters had begun to change; they were bleaker, more disjointed. And running through them all, this growing fear and hatred of one of his tutors: Dr Gareth Lacey. And then, finally, the phone call from her mother. She needed to come home. David was dead.

Davina had stood in the cemetery in Hastings, chilled to the very bone, and promised her brother that the man who'd put him into that deep dark hole would never get away with it. No matter what the cost. Well, she should have known that promises weren't always easy to keep. There would always be casualties when it came to revenge. And the round-faced, beaming principal of King Canute was one of them.

She watched him bleakly as he poured her the freshly made instant coffee and assured herself that the college would survive. They would all survive. She supposed even Gareth would survive. An ex-Oxford don would always be able to get a job somewhere, after all. He might go abroad, to America. But not into the education system, she thought, with a brief twist of her lips. His notoriety would travel even across the Atlantic. But the publishing world would probably welcome him. And this honest man, the principal, wouldn't be blamed for the actions of one of his students, would he?

Salving your conscience nicely, aren't you, Davina? she thought bitterly, and turned her attention to her coffee.

'Geoffrey Thorpe, our head of English, will be coming over when his class ends. I hope that's all right?' the principal said, and Davina smiled faintly, agreeing that it was.

The private investigator she'd hired was from London and came very highly recommended. She'd simply told him what she wanted — an English student at King Canute College, due to sit finals this summer, who looked set to fail, and who, as a result, wouldn't turn down the chance of earning an illicit few thousand. And, barely a week later, a list of four names, complete with biographies, had turned up in her pigeon-hole, together with a large bill. The list had included a single mother, who had to hold down a job as well as look after her son, and so had little time for study. Next on the list was an independently wealthy girl, who seemed to be using her time at college as a chance to drink, be merry and chase the male students in her year. The third name was that of a housewife and mother who'd decided to return to education and found things had changed so much since her own schooldays that she'd bitten off rather more than she could chew. And finally, there was a boy called Gavin Brock. From a middle-class family, he'd wasted his three years at the small college, being more interested in girlfriends, late nights and rock concerts than studying. He was counting on a cushy job in his father's company to set him up for life and was currently in a state of panic. Of them all, Brock was by far the best candidate.

'So, tell me what brings you to this neck of the woods,' the principal's voice penetrated her busy thoughts, and Davina forced herself to smile, to talk about the anthology, her Hilary Term as an honorary fellow at St Bede's, and her wish to lecture at some of the less well-endowed but equally deserving colleges within the state sector.

There was a knock on the door, and a thin, fair-haired man walked in. His watery blue eyes went straight to her.

'Ah, Geoffrey!' Mr Morgan bounced out of his chair and introduced them. 'Miss Granger, this is our head of English, Mr Thorpe. Miss Granger has just been telling me about an anthology she's compiling at St Bede's . . .'

Davina shook the man's hand, not surprised to find that her own hand was icy. Within half an hour, Davina had fixed a time and date, and was resolved to give them the best damned lecture she could think of. As she left, she could hear them happily discussing the local papers that must be informed, and once outside she checked her watch, relieved to see that it was just gone one o'clock.

She'd timed it perfectly. This time following her nose, she easily found her way to the college canteen, looking for one face in particular. Gavin Brock looked up as someone drew back a chair. He blinked as the blonde woman sat opposite him.

He blinked again, then smiled. 'Hello. I wouldn't have the pie if I were you.' He flashed her his best, charming, white-toothed grin.

Davina promptly smiled back. Fancied himself, didn't he? But she supposed he had good reason. At twenty-two, he was good-looking enough, in a very British sort of way. Dark hair, blue eyes, wide smile. 'I won't,' she promised, allowing her naturally soft voice to soften even more. 'You are Gavin Brock, aren't you?'

He swelled visibly. 'Sure. And you are . . . ?'

Davina, aware now of some of the openly interested looks being cast their way, rose slowly. 'Let's get out of here, shall we?' The smell of the food was beginning to nauseate her. 'It's nice outside,' she lied smoothly, 'and I'd like to talk to you . . . alone.'

Gavin had no problem with that and snatched his leather jacket off the back of the chair, following her out of the hot canteen like an eager puppy. Outside they both shivered as the raw March wind hit them, but neither complained. She began to lead him slowly away, towards the front gate.

In no mood, now they were alone, to indulge him in any more fantasies, she got straight to the point. 'How would you like to earn five thousand pounds?' she asked quietly.

Gavin jerked. 'Huh? What did you say?'

Davina smiled. 'I said,' she repeated patiently, 'how would you like to earn five thousand pounds?'

Gavin shoved his hands deep into his pockets and scowled at her, obviously unnerved.

Davina leaned against a wall and regarded him. 'Tell me, Gavin, what do you think your chances are of passing your finals this summer?' she asked casually.

The handsome waster grinned, a shade unconvincingly, at this sudden change in topic. He managed to shrug one shoulder nonchalantly. 'Piece of cake,' he boasted.

'Really? I thought your tutors had given you several written warnings that unless you bucked your ideas up, you were likely to get an unclassified.'

Gavin scowled, all sense of intrigue and sexual interest suddenly taking a nosedive. 'Here, are you a college trustee or something? Or did my old man send you?'

Davina laughed. 'Gavin, I have a proposition for you. You and I both know that you're about as likely to get your BA as I am to sprout wings and fly to Barbados. Right?' Gavin opened his mouth, about to deny it, then closed it just as quickly again. He sensed she was way out of his league. He'd begun to think of himself as a real ladies' man — a real man of the world. But just five minutes in the company of this woman, and he felt like a gauche schoolboy. Something about the catlike glint in those green eyes warned him that it wouldn't pay to play games with her.

'Yeah. That's right, I suppose,' he mumbled unwillingly.

Davina nodded. Good. This was going to work. She felt herself relax a little. 'Gavin, let's face it. You're between a rock and a hard place,' she said, her voice hardening now. 'You're due to leave here in the summer, just another student flooding the employment market without even a BA to show for it. Right?'

Gavin looked down at his feet. 'Yeah. I suppose that's about the size of it,' he admitted grudgingly.

'So, leaving here in June with a few thousand pounds to see you through until you can find something will be very handy, won't it?'

Gavin looked at her, something gleaming behind those bright eyes of his. He could take off. See the world. Backpack across America. Get out of the rat race.

Davina, recognising the gleam, smiled. 'Exactly. And that's what I'm offering you. Five thousand pounds — paid into the bank account of your choice. And all you have to do for it is do me a little favour.'

The gleam died. 'Do I look stupid, lady?' he said gruffly. 'I don't do drugs, or . . .'

Davina snarled. 'I'm not talking about drugs,' she snapped. 'I don't do drugs either.'

Gavin let out a long slow breath of relief. Then tensed again. 'It ain't legal though, is it?' he challenged. 'Nobody offers you five grand for something legal.'

Davina leaned back against the wall and shook her head. 'It's not, strictly speaking, a crime,' she said thoughtfully. 'You won't go to jail or anything like that.'

Gavin grunted. 'It will be messy though, won't it?'

'Oh yes,' she sighed wearily. 'It'll be messy all right.'

'So what do you want me to do?'

And there it was, Davina thought. The moment of truth. He was hooked. The trap was set. All she had to do was say the word . . . And she didn't want to. She knew the blankness of her mind might be permanent if she did. She might be destroying herself by destroying Gareth. She would hurt other people as well. She could simply walk away now, with only her own pain to contend with . . .

She turned and looked at Gavin Brock. 'I'm going to send you a copy of some of the papers that are in this year's finals. I want you to say that you gave Dr Gareth Lacey a thousand pounds for the copy. And that you know a lot of other students have done the same.'

* * *

Gareth lit the single red candle and stood back, his eyes sweeping over the table with a satisfied smile. He'd taken the delicate champagne flutes from the cabinet and brought a bottle of Bollinger from the fridge. He'd ordered in from a local restaurant salmon mousse, followed by a fresh seafood platter, with exorbitantly priced fresh strawberries and cream for dessert. The scouts, bless 'em, had provided him with a stiffly starched pure white linen tablecloth, the candle, and a little posy of primroses and tiny narcissus for a centrepiece. He went to the door and dimmed the lights, until the single candle flame flickered in the high-ceilinged, panelled room.

He was dressed in black trousers and a mint-green silk shirt, and when the knock came on the door he felt his heart leap into his throat.

He walked slowly across the Aubusson carpet, savouring every single heartbeat of anticipation. When he opened the door to her his breath caught somewhere between his sternum and his throat. She was wearing a white silk blouse, with no bra beneath. He could clearly see the outline of her breasts, and the dark aureoles of her nipples. He wondered if she'd worn the coat all the way across, or whether she'd taken it off as soon as she'd reached the hall in Walton. And, if she'd taken it off, whether any students had been coming or going.

With the sheer top, she was wearing a pair of lavender trousers, cut closely against her shapely thighs, but cropped an inch or two below her knees, giving her the look of a young and carefree girl. Long, dangling earrings of beaten gold disks almost touched her shoulders.

He opened the door further and let her in, still without speaking a word.

Davina walked into the room and stopped dead. In all the times she'd visited his rooms, she'd never seen it look like this. The candle, the flowers, the fire dancing merrily in the grate, the drawn curtains, the scent of narcissus wafting in the warm currents of air . . .

She kicked off her high-heeled shoes as she walked towards the table and stood looking down at it. 'Why all the trouble?' she asked softly, turning to look back at him. She had found his dinner invitation waiting for her when she'd returned, and decided she had no choice but to accept.

With the plan set, she had to stay close to him and make sure he walked into it.

Gareth too kicked off his shoes as he moved towards her, the rug feeling soft against his bare feet. 'It's a celebration,' he explained, his voice husky with emotion.

The candlelight highlighted the soft spikes of her hair, the point of her chin, the gleam of green eyes and the soft contours of her breasts beneath the silk. She looked like a conquering angel standing there — dangerous, beautiful, beguiling . . . He knew he'd never know another woman like her. Would never feel this depth of pain and pleasure again, this dizzying sensation of love and need and desire and uncertainty.

Davina was thinking of only hours ago. Of Gavin Brock's greed, and her own ruthlessness. Of the trap she'd set that would destroy this man . . .

'Davina,' he said, the agony and joy in his voice making her head whip round. He was walking towards her, drawing a small jeweller's box from his trouser pocket. Her heart lurched, threatened to stall. For one insane moment, she thought she was going to die, right here, right now, like a heroine from one of her poems, stricken down in her moment of betrayal. She swayed a little.

'The candle is for the candle in "The Flame Moth",' he whispered. 'You told me you'd finished it.'

Davina struggled to come back to reality. Blinked. '"The Flame Moth",' she whispered. 'Oh yes. I have.' She took a shaky breath. Fought for familiar ground. 'I decided that the metre I've chosen for my St Agnes verse is too steady, too regular. Have you ever seen a moth in flight in slow motion? It's all over the place . . . out of control . . . I thought I'd forget the pentameter and a syllable count . . .'

It was no good. Not when he was upon her now, the box opening, his storm-grey eyes bathing her, drowning her . . .

'Davina,' he said softly, and opened the box, displaying the most beautiful moth she'd ever seen. It had a lustrous grey pearl for its body, silver filigree wings studded with tiny diamonds, and sapphire eyes. She almost fainted.

Not a ring! Thank everything in creation, not a ring!

She swayed as he reached out to pin the exquisite, delicate brooch to the silk above her right breast. His fingers brushed the rounded curves beneath as he fastened it, and she gasped as her nipples burgeoned against the touch of his fingers. She swayed further towards him, like her moth had to its flame, falling against him, dragging him down with her on to the rug in front of the blazing fire. His lips clung to hers as he ran his fingers over her prominent cheekbones, learning the curves of her face like a blind man learns Braille.

She kissed him hungrily, desperately, her mind a blank no more, but filled with him. The sound, the sight, the romanticism of him. He was a man out of his time, she thought dizzily. He belonged in the age of Byron and Shelley.

'Gareth . . .' She pulled his mouth from hers, dragging his head to her breast. She felt his tongue flick out and caress her nipple through the silk. Her back arched as she held him against her, her head thrashing from side to side on the rug. She pushed the shirt from his skin, running her hands across his shoulders, loving the smooth warm flesh against her palms. They travelled over his back, to the indent at the base of his spine, and down, over the curved mounds of his tightly clenched buttocks. He gasped against her, raised his head to look down into her smoky green eyes.

'"The Flame Moth",' he said. 'It's for me, isn't it?' One part of him told him he was mad to take that for granted; that it was sheer arrogance to suppose that he was the inspiration behind it. Another part of him demanded she prove her love for him.

Davina thought of that poem she'd just finished — the hypnotic and glorious death that was the candle flame, the heroic, hopeless, singed moth . . . and nodded.

'Yes, Gareth,' she whispered huskily, tears coursing from her eyes now. 'It's for you.'

TEN

Davina leaned back against the Jaguar's cream leather uphol-
stery as they purred their way up the Woodstock Road.

'Where are we going?' she asked curiously, looking across
at Gareth, one delicately shaped eyebrow arched in enquiry.

'You'll see when we get there,' he murmured mysteriously and Davina smiled, enjoying the game. He was making
a big thing of this morning's adventure, but she was more
than content to let him. Last night, after he'd given her the
moth, was the first she'd spent sleeping in his arms. His bed
had been big and soft and warm, and the skin contact had
lulled her to sleep. This morning he'd brought her breakfast
in bed, and an invitation to accompany him on a mystery
tour.

His eyes strayed to her profile, and for once she looked
relaxed and even slightly sleepy. He drove north-west, towards
the Cotswolds, feeling at peace with the whole world.

He sighed deeply, the echo of last night's tender passion stirring gently in his bloodstream. He turned on the
radio and the car was filled with a diva singing about love,
and the man who was leaving her. Davina gave a small sigh
of bliss, as the scenery passed in a froth of white blackthorn
blossom.

Gareth, driving his fast car along a modern road, was a man with one foot firmly in the past — and he knew it. He loved the idea of a time when women and men had been prepared to kill, and die, for love. An age when men fought duels for a woman's honour. But he was no idle dreamer.

His career had been a great success, and he'd written volumes on Donne, Hunt, Keats and Brooke which graced practically every serious library in Britain, and beyond. Meeting, marrying and losing his wife, all in such a short period of time, had left him feeling burned out, wary and emotionally lost. Now, after all his years at St Bede's, he was wealthy, respected, confident, content. He was, by any criteria, a successful man. But it wasn't until this woman had come into his life, this wild, wonderful, savage, original creature called Davina Granger, that he realised that being safe was not what he needed. Not what he wanted any more.

No matter how cleverly he'd linked his passion for poetry with a pragmatic approach to life and career, he could no more back away from this wild, dangerous romance than he could turn lead into gold. Part of him understood that any kind of life with Davina Granger would be a life fraught with trouble. A roller-coaster ride that would leave him white-knuckled and holding on by his fingertips. But if he didn't join her on the merry-go-round, there would be no more evenings like last night. No more conversations like that very first one. No more mornings waking up, wondering what mad, bad, or dangerous thing she was going to do today.

'What are you thinking?' Davina suddenly asked softly, making him glance from the road and look across at her. She'd been watching him for some time now, fascinated by the subtle play of emotions criss-crossing his face.

She realised she loved his face. Those wings of dark hair, lifting gently in the breeze from the open window. Those deep, grey, mysterious eyes, with their fringe of dark lashes. The sharp nose. The firm lips. He wore tortoiseshell glasses when he read, she'd discovered yesterday. He had a way of being silent, and yet filling a space with his presence. He was all male and yet sensitive to the needs of others.

Gareth was proving to be . . . everything she'd ever wanted in a man. Which was annoying.

Although she was loath to admit it, she knew that Gareth Lacey was the one man she'd ever met who wouldn't try to tame her like a pet cat. The one man in the world who actually understood that poetry wasn't just what she wrote, but what she was. The one man who'd understand her mood swings and wouldn't get angry or bored with her mercurial temperament. And, now, the one man whose mind was always turning, underneath the calmness of his face, just as her own did.

'I want to know what you were thinking?' she said again, with just an edge of insistence in her voice now.

Gareth smiled. 'Nothing earth-shattering. I was just thinking how out of place I am in this modern world of ours,' he mused.

Davina's eyes narrowed. 'Are you? You seem to have it pretty much licked, as far as I can see. A cushy job. Respect,' she forced herself to choke the word out. 'Your choice of women. What more does a modern man want?'

Gareth frowned, surprised by her sudden venom.

'You sound as if you hate me,' he said quietly. He indicated left, leaving the dual carriageway, and heading towards the picturesque Cotswold village of Duns Tew.

'I do,' Davina said simply.

Gareth caught his breath.

She was wonderful.

'Good,' he said softly. 'Just as long as you're never indifferent.'

Davina fought back the urge to launch herself at him. Whether in attack, or to rip the clothes off him and ravish him, she wasn't quite sure. Any other man in the world would have been appalled by what she'd said. Would have been tongue-tied, or angry, or shell-shocked. But not this one.

'And I think I'm hating you more and more with every minute that passes,' she whispered.

Gareth, pulling up into a small, narrow lane, reached out and took her hand. He braked the car to a halt, switched off the engine, then turned in the seat, and looked into her stormy catlike eyes. 'Kiss me,' he commanded. And she did. Hard. Grinding her lips against his, forcing his head back against the leather headrest, their tongues duelling. Gareth felt his body leap as she clambered across the gear stick, her knees on either side of him, pressing herself firmly against him. He felt himself grow hard against her. She reached down for his zip, freeing him, dragging her own dress, a long, loose confection of tiny poppies against a cornflower blue sky, high up over her thighs. He groaned.

A car passed them, the driver giving them an astonished double-take.

Davina curled her hand around him. He felt so vulnerable in it. And yet so full of promising male power.

She felt his hips lift beneath her, but the car's bucket seat was too small and low-slung to allow him much room for manoeuvre. Lifting her head for a moment, she watched his eyes drift closed, heard a low, rumbling moan roll past his lips. She removed her hand and leaned back. His eyes snapped open. She glanced around them and smiled as a postman's van overtook them. Then she looked back at Gareth and shrugged graphically, her smudged lipstick making her look even more wild.

'We'll be seen,' she said regretfully.

'You don't care a damn if we're seen or not,' he shot back, his voice husky and dark.

'True.'

'You're just doing this to torture me,' he persisted.

Davina smiled. 'I know,' she leaned forward, her eyes only inches from his. 'Do you want me to stop?'

'No,' Gareth said softly. He swallowed hard. 'No. Never stop.'

Davina felt a sexual punch of desire hit her solidly in the very heart of her femininity. 'You're determined to be my soul mate, huh?' she whispered, eyes glittering.

'I *am* your soul mate.'

'What? The oh-so-respected, well-established Oxford don?'

Gareth leaned back in the seat, his body slowly, reluctantly, letting the clamour for release drain out of him as he realised she was not going to make love to him. He smiled gently. Whimsically. 'You don't like St Bede's?' he asked softly.

Davina laughed. 'Oh, it's all right. For what it is. But I wouldn't want to live there for ever.'

'No. Neither would I,' he said. And took her utterly by surprise, both with his strength of body, and strength of mind, when he shifted her up off his lap in a one-armed lift and thrust her to one side. He zipped himself up, got out of the car, and then walked around to her side, gallantly opening her own door for her. Bemused, Davina slid out. 'Which is why,' Gareth continued, turning around and holding out a hand towards the building opposite them, 'I've bought this place.'

Davina looked long and hard into his face for one endless moment, then turned to view the cottage in question.

It was on the very edge of the village. A simple, classic, thatched Cotswold cottage, made of pale Cotswold stone, gleaming like clotted cream in the spring sunshine. The thatch had been renewed last year, she could see, and was the indeterminate colour of straw weathered to a tan brown. The windows were low, ancient, and newly painted white. The door was set straight as an arrow in the very centre of the building. A chimney stood at one end. Surrounded by a drystone wall, the garden was already frothing with spring colour, from early wallflowers to blue and pink hyacinths.

'How very . . . pretty,' she said. And it was. They walked across the road to the gate, which opened with a teeth-tingling squeak.

He moved in front of her, extracting a set of keys from his pocket, and opened the door, his eyes slightly mocking as he ushered her inside. The door opened straight into the living room itself. Genuine low oak beams ran the length the ceiling. The ancient walls bulged and were painted an off-white. A stone fireplace dominated one wall.

'I do hope you weren't thinking of polka-dot curtains and floral chair covers,' Davina muttered drolly over one shoulder, as he marched inside and looked around.

'No. I thought I'd leave the decorating to you.'

The words echoed in the cool empty interior, bouncing off the walls and ricocheting back to her, making her eyes widen.

She turned, slowly, and looked at him. Gareth closed the door behind him, the old-fashioned black-painted latch falling and enclosing them in a cool private silence.

'Me? Why should I decorate the place?'

Gareth continued to look at her. His eyes were as fathomless as the ocean, and as powerful. 'Don't you want to?' he challenged her softly.

Davina turned away quickly, before he could decipher the look on her face. She turned, looking around the empty room. Being black and white, it cried out for loud, bold splashes of colour. Ruby-red velvet curtains, perhaps, or scarlet silk? A leather couch in front of the fireplace. A bold, multi-coloured Arabic rug on the floor. And around the lights . . . stained-glass? She knew a woman who made exquisite stained-glass lampshades. She moved towards the empty fireplace, imagining a log fire flickering away.

'Are you asking me to move in with you?' she asked loftily, looking at the soot-darkened stones.

'Yes.'

'You know I'm not the home-making type.'

'A real home doesn't need to be made,' Gareth mused. 'It just is.'

Davina laughed. 'You should write greeting-card verses,' she said, deliberately cruel. She turned then, to see what effect she'd had on him, and instantly saw that it was none at all. He was still leaning against that door, still looking wonderful, still watching her with that patient, considering, gentle understanding. Damn him!

She turned back to the fireplace, tossing her fine blonde head, wondering what the hell she thought she was doing.

Wasn't this everything she could hope for?

She had part two of her plan well under way. As soon as he'd finished setting those exam papers, all she had to do was make a photocopy. Pay off Gavin Brock. And then sit back and watch Gareth's world fall apart. And now, right here, he was offering her another way to break his heart. He was asking her to share this place with him. His dream cottage. His life. What better way to teach him what real pain betrayal could cause? So why was she hesitating? Why wasn't she reassuring him that of course she would decorate this beautiful place for him. Of course she would come live with him and be his love . . .

'It can be on any terms that you want,' Gareth said quietly, watching her shoulders tense, as if he'd just issued a threat rather than a freedom. 'If you want to go back to London and only come here for the odd weekend, that's all right. Or stay away for longer and come for a few weeks at a time. Or just come in between jaunts to wherever in the world you want to visit,' he murmured, 'I don't mind. So long as you come home to me.'

He'd read the poems she'd written while she'd been in Borneo, living in a beach hut. Poems written in the Australian Outback. Poems written when she'd been in Hollywood, living with Jax Coulson. He understood that inspiration meant everything . . .

'That's very obliging of you,' Davina said drolly, trying to put some venom into her voice and failing miserably. 'Like being a doormat, do you?'

Gareth sighed deeply. 'It's not going to work, Davina, I told you that,' he said quietly. 'You only have the power to treat me like a doormat if I choose to give you that power. And I don't.'

She turned on him then, her cat-green eyes blazing. 'Oh, but in the meantime, I have your permission to come and go from this place, just how I like?'

'Yes.'

'Living just as I please?' Her chin lifted challengingly.

'Yes.'

'And what if I decide to take a new lover as well?'

Gareth's eyes flickered. He felt the room around him recede, then rush back. Felt pain. Anger. Fear. And then, suddenly, as clear as a flash from a precious gem, he understood a truth that had his heart melting. 'You don't do infidelity, Davina,' he reminded her quietly.

Davina felt her eyes widen. How . . . She turned back to the fireplace. 'You know me pretty well, don't you?' she said bitterly.

Gareth moved from the door at last, walking across the empty floor, his footsteps echoing eerily off the walls. She tensed, then relaxed, as his arms slipped around her. His hands folded across her waist, pulling her back, nestling the curve of her spine against the line of his chest and stomach.

They fitted like a pair of spoons.

'Yes, I do,' he said softly. 'That scares you, doesn't it?'

Davina smiled ruefully. It did, somewhat! 'You're a strange man, Gareth Lacey,' she said at last. 'Tell me about that student who died.' She blinked, wondering where those words had come from. She hadn't even been thinking about David. And yet . . . Yes. She had to know. Now, before she could say yes or no to moving into this cottage with him. She had to have his version of the death of her brother.

Gareth stiffened, and almost instantly pushed her away. She sensed at once the upheaval inside him and turned to watch him walk to one of the windows and stare out across the rolling Oxfordshire countryside. 'What do you want to know?' he asked bleakly.

'Why did he die?'

'He killed himself.'

Davina clenched her hands into fists and forced them open again. He sounded so . . . blank. As if the words he was saying meant nothing. 'Why?'

'I caught him cheating on his prelims.'

'How can you be so sure that he cheated?' she demanded angrily, knowing that David would never cheat in his life.

Gareth turned to look at her, the grey eyes genuinely puzzled. 'Why do you want to talk about all this, Davina?' he asked, his voice dangerously soft, and she felt a warning shaft of alarm flicker through her. Damn, she should have known not to push him too hard. She'd always known she would have to keep a tight rein on her feelings.

If he began to suspect . . . She shrugged. 'Oh, you know all about Jax Coulson, who has to be the biggest disaster in my life. I just wanted to know about your secret too.'

Gareth shook his head. 'What do I know about Jax Coulson? You were together when he was a struggling actor, you split up when he made it big. He gave a rather lurid interview about you that made you sound like a human version of a black widow spider, and you kept quiet.' He shrugged.

Davina laughed. 'Jax was . . . a man with a dream when I met him,' she began to explain.

'You loved him?' he asked curiously.

'Not like I love you.'

Davina would have taken the words back the moment they left her mouth, came out of her subconscious, but it was too late.

Gareth couldn't say a word. Couldn't think of a word that would fit. He just . . . lived the most wonderful moment of his life.

'When he made it big, the fame just . . . went straight to his head. So I ended it.'

'He was angry? That was why he dumped on you so publicly?'

Davina shook her head, laughing softly. 'Hell no. It was his publicist who put him up to that interview and gave him the famous quote. I didn't mind. I am wild.'

'I love you.'

She stared into the fireplace. 'I know.'

'Davina?' he said softly.

'What?'

'Why don't you think we stand a chance?'

The quick gasp she gave was easily audible in the fraught quietness of the empty room. So, he'd picked up on that had he? Why was she so surprised? She turned around slowly. Looked at him. And wanted to tell him the truth. *We're doomed, my darling, because you killed my brother.*

It was as if they were living in some hideous scene from *Romeo and Juliet!* She wanted to laugh, and cry. But she did neither. 'Perhaps I just don't trust you enough yet.'

Gareth nodded. 'Time will cure that,' he said confidently. And it would. She would come to learn that being loved didn't have to mean being controlled. Being caged.

Time. Davina laughed. Time would only show him that you couldn't destroy people and get away with it. That's all that time would show her soul mate Gareth Lacey.

She laughed again, a bleak, harsh bark of laughter, but Gareth wouldn't have traded it for a gentler kind from a gentler woman.

Davina was his. Claws, complications, contradictions and all.

He wouldn't have it any other way.

ELEVEN

Jared rubbed a hand wearily across his forehead as the red curtains got stuck halfway across the stage. Beside him, Alicia grinned. 'It'll be all right on the night,' she muttered, sotto voce. 'At least we've ironed out the problems in the play; spotlights that don't work and all the rest of it are just technical hitches, aren't they?'

Jared leaned one arm along the back of her chair. 'So that's the way it is?' he drawled. 'My play's all right, so all the nitty-gritty little problems are your headache!' Alicia laughed, but was acutely aware of his every movement. The way his T-shirt clung to his muscles and fluttered at the neck with every breath he took. The scent of his aftershave. The touch of his breath on her cheek. Since that kiss in the punt, she seemed to feel uneasy whenever Jared was around.

'Right, you lot can go,' Jared called. 'We'll go for a full dress rehearsal tomorrow. Props! Did you hear that?' From the colourful language that filtered back to him, he assumed props had heard all right. Alicia grinned as the room emptied. Sin-Jun was throwing a small party in the SCR in honour of her brother, and they were all invited.

'Aren't you all a-flutter at being invited into the mysterious depths of the Senior Common Room?' he teased, lifting one finger to trace the curve at the nape of her neck.

At his touch, a wonderful but very physical tingle shot down her spine and she dragged in a quick gasp of air.

Jared, who was watching his finger curl a long lock of raven hair around it, smiled whimsically. He might be wrapping her around his little finger in this aspect, but as things went . . .

He was the one completely in her thrall. Her shyness, and the way she battled to overcome it, charmed him. Her growing confidence, in both her play and her ability to write, made him want to burst into song. Ever since that day in the punt, he'd been longing to kiss her again, but he wanted it to be special. A woman like Alicia should be wooed. With flowers, and walks in the park, and romantic candlelit dinners and . . .

'So, I expect you're nervous about next term, hm?' Alicia, who'd been wracking her brains for something intelligent to say, was somewhat entranced by the hand still on her neck.

'What?' Jared croaked. 'Oh, you mean finals. Yes, I suppose so. But I hope to get a first. Arrogant so-and-so, aren't I?'

Alicia laughed. She loved him when he was laughing at himself. Loved him when he was smiling. Just . . . loved him.

Now, having him all to herself in the quietness of the dark theatre, she wanted to take the opportunity to learn every last thing about him. From his favourite colour, down to the way he liked to clean his teeth.

'What'll you do when you leave here?' she asked, a pang of pain lancing through her as she realised how very close that day was. Just one short term . . .

Jared shrugged. 'I've already applied to do a BSc in Engineering. I'll need it if I'm to get a job with the firm I want.' He named a very prestigious firm indeed. One that regularly won contracts to build roads and dams and bridges all over the globe. 'A BA from Oxford won't be enough to get me in,' he stated matter-of-factly. 'Not even a first. A BA and a BSc might, though,' he added.

'And . . . which college are you applying to?' she asked, trying not to sound too pathetic as she held her breath for the answer.

'I'm staying here, of course. You think I want to go somewhere else when you're here?'

Her breath rushed out of her in a very audible sigh. Then she blushed. He must have heard it! Quick! Think of something to say! 'What do your parents think of it all?'

Jared stirred restlessly and let her hair fall free from his fingers. Taking her courage in her hands, Alicia turned sideways to face him.

Their faces were now only inches apart. This time it was Jared who noticed the rise and fall of her breasts beneath the cotton sweater. The scent of her floral perfume wafting towards him. The sweet curve of her unpainted lips as she smiled . . . 'Hm? Oh, they're happy. Dad's got a good job, so they won't object to me still not earning,' he grinned.

It gave Alicia a bit of a jolt. Stupid, of course, to just imagine everyone in the world was as comfortably placed as the Normans. Jared saw the surprise and then chagrin cross her face, and bit back the fear that began to gnaw at him.

When they were working on the play together it was easy to forget the vast differences in their backgrounds. Then, like now, he'd suddenly see himself through her eyes.

'You come from Bicester, don't you?' she named the small market town in north Oxfordshire.

He nodded. 'That's right. I was brought up in a nice little council house on a nice little estate.' He knew he was being facetious. Knew he should shut up. It wasn't her fault that she knew nothing about his world. Why should she?

Alicia sensed only the sudden pain in him. The sudden conflict. 'Jared?' she said softly. 'What's wrong with a council house?'

He closed his eyes briefly, then opened them again. 'Nothing. Nothing's wrong with it. It's just . . . I never want to go back there. Oh, I don't mean literally. I mean . . . I want to go forward. To something different.'

She leaned closer, a slightly puzzled look creasing her lush dark brows, but a thirst for understanding in her china-blue eyes. 'Tell me,' she said softly.

And so he did. Holding nothing back. 'When I was growing up, I went to a tough school. The corridors were always full of roving gangs of bullies, the classrooms were in concrete blocks that were freezing in winter, not enough textbooks. Everything about it depressed me. But even then, at the age of thirteen, I could see that the school was my only chance.'

He looked at her, wishing . . .

'Chance for what?' she prompted, although she already knew the answer.

'A chance to do something with my life other than get a dead-end job, or . . . go to jail. Like my brother,' he said starkly, watching her closely now.

Alicia was shocked. She knew she shouldn't be. She knew, utterly logically, that what someone's brother did, or was, was no reflection on them. Hadn't Neville's presence here already told her that? But she was shocked. She couldn't help it.

She'd never even known anybody who'd gone to jail. Or known somebody who'd known somebody who'd gone to jail.

'Yes,' Jared said frankly, almost uncannily reading her mind. 'My older brother's in jail. For burglary. He watched others swanning around in fancy cars and thought the world owed him a living. Of course, the world didn't think so.' Now that he'd begun, he was determined to be ruthlessly honest. With both himself, and with her. Alicia deserved no less.

'When I got into Oxford, and having gained an exhibition, Mum and Dad were thrilled, but they didn't really understand what I was doing here.'

'I want to meet them,' she said softly. And she did. They sounded wonderful.

'You will,' Jared promised huskily. 'Mind, I'm not try-ing to make myself into some kind of saint,' he laughed, a touch embarrassed now. 'I'm in this for the money,' he said drolly. 'I want to get rich. One day, start my own company. Be one of those fat-cat company chairmen.'

'A chairman who still goes out to Colombia in his hard hat and designs bridges though,' she said softly. Her eyes were luminous now, glowing like Ceylon sapphires in the dark-ness of the theatre, and Jared caught his breath. She had him pegged. Right down to his last dream . . . He could see the ado-ration in her eyes. But wanted more. Something much more lasting than that. She was so young still . . . It made him afraid.

'Alicia,' he said softly. 'You know, Agatha Christie trav-elled all over the world with that archaeologist husband of hers. You could come to Colombia with me. Write about a murder on a construction site.'

She wondered if he was joking. Or if he really meant . . . could possibly mean . . . could actually be asking her to go with him. To stay with him.

'Jared,' she said softly, but he was already leaning across to her. The hand, which had played so gently with a tendril of her hair, now suddenly cupped the back of her skull, drawing her closer to him. She just had time to draw in a quick breath, close her eyes, and then his lips were on hers. Gentle at first, then moving with a growing hunger. He pulled her closer, dragging her half on to his lap. She felt the hard firmness of his thighs against her own. Her arms came around him, linking behind his neck, her breasts pressed close to him. He moaned, leaning back in the seat, until he and Alicia were sprawled across three of the front-row seats. Jared could feel an armrest pressing painfully against his back but ignored it.

She was lying on top of him, the curtain of her raven hair spilling over them, enclosing them in a dark, secret place, where their lips met, and their minds fused, and their bodies pulsated against one another. They were in a private world, a creation of their own making. She ran her hand down over his ribs, into the indentation of his waist and then across his sensitive stomach, which shuddered at the teasing play of her fingers. He felt his calf muscles jerk as she moved one of her knees, accidentally brushing against the hardness of his shaft underneath the jeans.

He moaned again. Alicia had never felt such power over a man. Or such lack of control over herself. She lifted her lips, saw the pale gleam of the skin at the base of his throat, and before even thinking about it, dipped her mouth to press her lips against him there. Her tongue flickered out, tracing a path across his skin. It tasted slightly salty. And warm. And of something that was indefinably and *only* Jared.

Jared moaned again. His head fell back against the next seat, and his throat arched. Alicia watched entranced, her eyes tracing the cords in his tense neck, following the dance of his Adam's apple as he swallowed in compulsive gulps. Her legs moved between his, forcing them apart. Against her abdomen, she suddenly felt the hardness of him. It sent a ripple of shock, then of desire, lancing through her. He wanted her. No matter what else he was thinking. No matter how he saw her or the relationship — a quick affair or a long-term lover — right here and now, he wanted her. And, suddenly, it was enough. Any trace of prudery left her, burned away by the alchemy that was mutual desire.

Alicia bit his earlobe gently. Felt him shudder. Her lips trailed across that vulnerable throat, tracing the pulse which beat there so erratically, and felt him begin to shake. She . . .

'Is anyone in here? Alicia?'

The voice came from the doorway to the theatre, and it brought with it a blast of cold air. With a muffled squeak of embarrassment, Alicia shuffled backwards, sitting upright, her face flaming. She hoped the darkness hid a multitude of sins.

'Emily? Is that you?' she managed to get out, her voice wavering wildly. She staggered to her feet.

Her knees felt like jelly.

Emily peered into the darkness as her friend began to walk up the centre aisle. 'Where's Jared? The party in the SCR is about to begin. Rupert's fretting that you aren't there.'

Alicia managed to smile as she stepped into the daylight pouring in through the open door. 'Oh? Well, I'll be right along. Jared . . .' she cleared her throat, 'Jared left a while ago. I dare say he'll be along soon.'

Emily wasn't fooled for one moment. Her friend had the rosy glow of a woman who'd just been seduced. Her eyes were almost glowing. Emily shot an amused glance into the darkened theatre, but very prudently hid a grin. 'Right. Are you going to change?'

'Of course,' Alicia muttered.

In the darkness, Jared heard the door shut, the echo bouncing around him. He groaned again, loud and long, his hands clenching into fists by his side. He was on fire! Although he would always love Emily for introducing him to Alicia and being his ally in his fight to win her, right at that moment he could cheerfully have strangled her!

Sin-Jun beamed as Neville Norman accepted a sherry from the butler and continued to regale Gareth Lacey with a hilarious tale about a play he'd reviewed at the Globe.

Rupert Greyling-Simms stood alone, waiting for Alicia. When she did finally arrive, she was wearing a plain, soft cream dress that fell in gentle folds to just below her knees. A flower was embroidered across the left shoulder of the dress, with leaves which trailed across her breast and over her waist. With it she wore a simple gold chain, and gold stud earrings. Plain, low-heeled cream shoes and pale tights completed the outfit.

Elegant and understated. Everything about her screamed class. Screamed refinement. Screamed 'lady'.

Neville pulled his sister effortlessly into his orbit.

Gareth murmured a discreet excuse, nodded to Sin-Jun, and made his way to the door. He was meeting Davina for lunch, and then going on to Woodstock with her. She was helping him tour the antique shops to pick out furniture for the cottage.

Rupert glided towards brother and sister.

'You're late,' Neville murmured to her, careful to keep his voice down. 'I didn't think you were ever coming.'

'I had to make notes.'

Neville didn't like the glitter of repressed excitement in her eyes. Every time he came to Oxford, his sister seemed to have changed just a little bit more, and he was determined to put her straight. Nineteen was such a dangerous age. She could ruin her life so easily.

'I hope that director of yours has been giving you a wide berth,' he said casually. 'After paying the man ten thousand to leave you alone, I would hate to think he was reneging on our agreement.'

Rupert, overhearing, also heard Alicia gasp, and it made him wince. He'd suspected, of course, that she was infatuated with Jared Cowan. But then, she was young, inexperienced. It was a good thing that Alicia had a brother like Neville to protect her. He needed to take home an unblemished bride.

Alicia stared blankly at Neville. 'Paid . . . ?' she whispered, her mind struggling to find its footing again. She felt as if she'd just wandered off some precipice. 'You . . . paid . . . Jared to . . .'

'Leave you alone,' Neville supplied for her helpfully. 'Yes I did. And he laughed as he took it,' he finished briskly. There, it was done. Perhaps now she'd see sense.

Alicia simply didn't believe it. She gave her brother a narrow-eyed look. 'I think you're lying,' she said flatly. She turned, trying to spot Jared, but before she could, Rupert suddenly stepped right in front of her.

'Hello, darling,' he murmured, reaching across to kiss her cheek, and Alicia accepted it as the kind of polite social etiquette that meant nothing. She barely registered the touch of his lips. Instead, her eyes gazed past his shoulder . . . Where was Jared? To the others in the room, however, that murmured endearment and kiss seemed to blaze a huge sign across the room. Members of the cast, who'd begun to assume that Alicia and Jared were an item, suddenly found themselves hastily revising their ideas.

Emily glanced across to see whether Jared had noticed, and realised, from his frozen stance, that he had.

Neville beamed. 'Rupert. So good to see you again. Alicia, I've been hearing from the others that Rupert's the star of the show.'

It was no good. With Rupert standing squarely in front of her, she couldn't see Jared anywhere. 'Hm? What? Oh yes, he makes a wonderful killer.'

What a joy she was. Rupert laughed. He leaned forward. 'I hope that was meant as a compliment.' He placed a hand on her arm as he smiled.

Rupert, she'd noticed, seemed to need praise and reassurance far more than any other member of the cast. She reached out and squeezed his arm. 'You'll be fine.'

Noticing Jared Cowan weaving his way towards them, Rupert recognised that determined look on his face at once. He turned quickly to Alicia. 'I'm going back to Warrington Manor next weekend. My father's giving a party. I was wondering if you'd like to come?'

Neville knew all about the Warrington March Ball. It was the social event of the year in the county. He beamed. 'How wonderful of you to ask, Rupert. Of course Alicia would be delighted to come. Won't you, Alicia?' He, too, had sensed a presence bearing down on them, and didn't need to look around to know who it was.

Alicia's eyes suddenly met those of Jared. He'd seemed to come from out of nowhere. Her eyes searched his. It was impossible to think he had accepted money from her brother . . .

And then she wondered. Perhaps he had taken it, just to thumb his nose at them at all. He'd been so open and honest about his desire to earn money . . . Perhaps that had been his way of warning her . . . No. She was being ridiculous. Of course Jared, her Jared, wouldn't . . .

'Alicia?' Neville said sharply. 'Rupert's waiting for an answer. To his invitation,' he added, staccato-voiced now. She was going to blow it if she wasn't careful. Invitations to the Warrington Ball were like gold dust.

Alicia dragged her eyes back to Rupert. After all, looking at his smooth blond handsomeness was far easier than looking at Jared and wondering . . . 'Oh. Yes, of course. Thank you, I'd love to come to your party.'

'Splendid,' Rupert beamed. 'I'll pick you up Friday then. We'll drive down and come back Sunday afternoon.' Alicia was surprised to find she'd just agreed to a whole weekend at Warrington Manor. Then she saw Jared turn away, a strange look in his eye, and felt her heart sink. She reached for another glass of sherry and tried valiantly to tell herself that her heart was not breaking.

TWELVE

Davina tapped on Gareth's door. She was wearing a long white cotton dress she'd picked up in a little second-hand shop just off St Aldates. As she entered, Gareth looked up from his desk. His eyes took in the vision in white walking towards him, and he felt his pulse flutter. Her sense of style was just one of the many things that made her unique.

'Davina,' he said simply, and walked to a small drinks cabinet, bringing out, unasked, a bottle of elderflower champagne. 'I got this a few weeks ago. Want some?'

'Love some,' Davina murmured as he reached for a pair of tall, fluted glasses that he'd kept in the fridge. She accepted the cold glass and bubbling golden liquid, her spirit expanding. When he linked arms around hers, so that their faces were close together, she felt a deep sense of well-being. She'd never met a more romantic man than Gareth Lacey.

'Mmm,' she murmured. 'The taste is . . . ethereal.'

'I know. It's like drinking bottled sunshine.'

'Or flavoured raindrops.'

'You always have to have the last word?'

'One-upmanship was invented just for me.'

'And you're so good at it.'

Davina inclined her head gracefully. 'Thank you.' Gareth smiled. He loved tussling with her. Not to see who won — that was irrelevant. Sometimes he did, sometimes she did. No, it was just the tussling in itself that sharpened his reflexes and gave him a reminder of how alive he was beginning to feel.

'Just let me file this stuff away,' he murmured, putting down his glass and reaching across the desk for some student essays. He walked to a filing cabinet, unlocked it, and began to riffle his way through it. Idly, Davina sat on the edge of his desk, and swung one foot lazily to and fro. As she sipped her elderflower wine, she glanced down, her eyes falling on to his desk diary. And her heart jumped.

Monday of next week was circled in red, and in his sloping, almost copperplate handwriting, was the message: *Exam papers deadline. Must post by today.*

She glanced at his back thoughtfully. He was wearing a plain cotton white shirt, and it clung to his back in places, where he'd been sitting pressed against the back of his chair. She could see the smooth planes of his flesh underneath. His head was bent, a lock of dark hair falling enticingly across his forehead as he searched his files for the names of the two young men who'd just left, and Davina found herself instinctively longing to brush the strands back so that she could discover the secrets hidden in his eyes. Just why had this man, of all men, become so antagonistic towards David?

It was a question, unbelievably, that she'd never asked herself before. And since coming to St Bede's, she was beginning to find it more and more difficult to reconcile the man she'd found with the man of her imagination.

Stalking a man was one of the most intimate things she'd ever done. She was getting under his skin. Drilling a way into his mind. Ferreting in his psyche. And, after just a little more than a month, she knew Gareth Lacey better than any lover she'd ever had. And what she knew didn't seem to make sense. He found the files, shut the cabinet, carefully locked it again, and turned back to her.

The grey eyes again. She knew as long as she lived she'd never forget those unique grey eyes of his.

'You look miles away.'

'I was,' she admitted. Just what had made him hate David?

'So,' Gareth said, walking towards her, his hands thrust deep in the pockets of his jeans, 'do you want to eat out?'

Davina smiled. 'I'd love to.'

'Where shall we go?'

'Surprise me,' she demanded challengingly.

He gave her a long level look, then nodded. 'OK.' He got his jacket and checked for his wallet. 'I'll be right back.'

She watched him go, her eyes still thoughtful, her mind on David. She heard an impatient drumming sound and realised that she'd been unconsciously drumming her fingers restlessly against the side of his desk for some time now. It was a sure sign of inner agitation. She forced herself to relax. To close her eyes. To think.

From David's letters it was clear that his tutor, Gareth Lacey, had only slowly become hostile towards him. Had *gradually* become sarcastic and bitter towards him. Had, over the course of her brother's last two terms in Oxford, shown signs of personal antipathy. So what did that indicate?

Had David produced such brilliant work that the great Gareth Lacey had found himself threatened? She sighed. Much as she adored her brother, she knew him to be no academic genius. Whereas Gareth Lacey was.

It was no good. She just couldn't think why Gareth had turned vindictive. But he had driven David to suicide.

The door opened, and Gareth returned.

'You're empty-handed,' she said, with deliberate self-irony. It made two of them.

'It's in the car. I thought we'd go for a picnic.'

'Oh? Where?'

He smiled mysteriously. 'You'll see.'

She followed him out to the car park, sliding into the Jaguar XJS, her white dress flowing neatly around her ankles.

He drove them out of Oxford, through Kidlington and up the main road that led towards Banbury. For a while she was uncomfortable, thinking that he was taking her to King Canute College. That, somehow, he'd found out what she was doing. That this was all a cleverly laid trap. It made her heart beat faster, with a combination of both fear and excitement.

Half of her wished he did know. It would make the fight more fair. While she had no compunction about destroying this man as he deserved, the thought of doing it sneakily, an ambush, had never truly sat easily with her. She was by nature a fighter. A face-to-face combatant.

But halfway up the Oxford-to-Banbury road, he indicated right, taking her down into a beautiful valley of the River Cherwell.

'Where are we?' she asked, as they crossed a bridge, and a big grey house appeared on a rise to their right.

'Rousham House,' Gareth told her.

Davina saw the road sign that told them they were approaching the village of Lower Heyford. They'd just driven up and over a humped railway bridge when he suddenly indicated left, into an almost concealed entrance that led to a boat yard. Davina gasped in delight, suddenly finding herself facing a line of gaily painted narrowboats. She got out of the car, her heart lifting at the sight of the river craft. Their own traditional artwork was reflected in the panels of painted flowers, castles, rivers and birds that bedecked their hulls.

'Wait here a moment,' Gareth told her, and she walked to the canal edge, reading some of the names of the moored blue and yellow boats. *King Alfred*, *Dylan Thomas* and, more comically, *Toe Rag*. Their roofs were lined with tubs of gaily flowering polyanthus, pansies and jonquils.

Gareth came back, retrieved a picnic basket from the boot of the Jag, and led her to the far end of the jetty. There, a pretty little barge, painted pale blue, cream and green, bobbed gently in the water. She read the name painted on the bow: *Halcyone*.

'The kingfisher,' she mused out loud.

Gareth nodded. 'Wasn't she the maid who turned herself into a kingfisher to escape being seduced by Zeus?' he murmured. 'The ancient Greeks certainly had a fascinating mythology.' He produced the key and opened the small doors that led down into the dark, narrow interior.

'She's ours until four o'clock,' he said, watching her as she walked quickly through the tiny rooms, drawing back the curtains as she went, letting the daylight flood in. He cast off and started the engine, expertly manoeuvring the boat out into the canal.

She emerged on to the deck, watching him steer the boat. 'Looks simple, doesn't it?' Gareth told her. 'But if you want to go left, you have to turn the rudder right, and vice versa. And you have to do it a good way in advance.'

The engine was so quiet she could hardly hear it. 'How fast are we going?' she asked curiously. It seemed they were barely at walking pace.

Gareth sighed blissfully. 'There's a four-mile-an-hour speed limit on the canal,' he said, and laughed.

Davina, who was used to living her life at a much faster pace, laughed too. 'It's bliss,' she agreed, watching two donkeys in a field lift their heads to watch them drift by, idle interest on their sweet faces. A church tower came and went. They rounded a bend and found weeping willows, gardens full of daffodils, a pair of marauding ducks, and a white drawbridge awaiting them.

'Someone's going to have to get off and raise it,' Gareth said dryly. 'It's too low for us to get under.'

'Hm,' Davina murmured, giving him a jaundiced look. 'And since you're steering, it's going to have to be me, right?' she hazarded.

Gareth grinned. 'I thought you were never going to volunteer.' He steered the boat to the towpath's edge, and she walked carefully along the very narrow rim of the boat, leaping off on to the grass when there was still nearly a foot of water between it and the boat. Gareth watched the graceful flying leap with his heart in his mouth. The long white dress lifted in the breeze as she flew through the air, revealing long, slim legs. She landed lightly, and sprinted easily along the towpath, crossing the bridge and eyeing it carefully. A long grey chain hung from one of the two metal arms, and she shrugged and pulled on it. The bridge lifted easily. When *Halcyone* was through, she carefully lowered the bridge behind her again and got back aboard.

She could get used to this sort of life. For a while.

The sun, which had been shining brightly all day, was at its zenith now, and Davina climbed lithely on to the roof. There she walked fearlessly across the top of it, before sitting down, kicking off her shoes, and leaning back on her hands, her face turned up to the sun. In her long white dress she looked like some pagan priestess, Gareth thought. And wished he could write a poem to her. Then his lips twisted at the inanity of the thought. No. Davina *was* a poem. A poet. She needed no such homage from him.

They entered the lock at Upper Heyford a quarter of an hour later, Davina quickly mastering the use of the lock key, and just past a pretty redbrick canal bridge he moored the boat to the side. It being March, not many people were indulging in a boating holiday, and they had the canal to themselves. A big bush of pussy-willow, with its fat, lemon, pollen-saturated flowers, showered them with a gentle golden mist as the slight breeze rustled through it.

Gareth hoisted the hamper on to the top of the canal barge and sprawled out next to Davina. He opened the basket and peered inside.

'Don't tell me,' she sighed, still with her head tilted up towards the warm sun. 'Smoked salmon, oysters, and Italian bread.'

'Close,' Gareth murmured. 'Pork pie, beer, and cheese that's strong enough to get up and walk off by itself.'

She laughed, and watched him bring out exactly that, along with some fresh fruit.

The beer came from a local brewery in Chipping Norton, and she drank it straight from the bottle. He reached for a taste, but she swung the bottle out of his reach. 'If you're a good boy I'll let you kiss me.'

'Generous to a fault, aren't you?' Gareth mused, then sat up. 'Look!' he pointed to a flash of turquoise and orange flitting past them. 'A real kingfisher.'

Davina too shot up, just in time to see the streak of blue dash around the bend in the canal and disappear. When she turned back, Gareth was swallowing the beer. She cast doubts on his ancestry in very modern language, then helped herself to some fruit.

When the hamper was empty at last, and Gareth had carefully lowered it on to the rear deck of the boat, she slowly lay back against the roof, the painted surface warm to her spine.

She saw the shadow that could only be Gareth's loom against her closed lids, blocking out the light from the sun.

For a while she let the play of colours dance across her lids. Orange. Blazing green. Deep blue. Then she opened her eyes.

Stormy eyes looked back.

'I suppose you want me now?' she said softly.

Gareth smiled. Reached out a finger to trace the line of her jaw. 'I always want you,' he admitted softly. 'From the first moment I saw you. Now. And I'll still be wanting you when my last moment comes.'

She sighed softly. 'Gareth.'

'What?'

She thought of David. She thought of herself. She thought of him. She thought, . . . I'm in trouble.

'Nothing,' she murmured. 'Come here.'

She pulled him down on top of her, taking his hand and guiding it to her left breast. She sighed softly as his fingers curled around the curve of her flesh there, and moaned sensuously, softly, as his thumb brushed hard against her burgeoning nipple. It was a slow, lazy, fluid kind of love that they made that afternoon. He didn't remove her flowing white dress, just pulled the hem up to her waist. With only the slightest trace of her former tan remaining, she looked, he thought drowsily, breathlessly, like a woman made of milk and honey. And he laughed at himself, because he wasn't fooled by the disguise.

He buried himself in her, and caught fire, losing himself in the ecstasy of the moment. Once, he called out her name, and startled a pair of moorhens who were busy building a nest in a patch of reeds on the neighbouring riverbank.

Afterwards, Davina lay staring up at the sky. His head was pillowed against her breast, and she was absently stroking the damp, dark hair back from his face. She could feel the contours of the bones of his skull, cheek and jaw under her fingers. Could feel the heavy thud of his heartbeat slowing to normal against her own, racing heart. Could feel the coolness of the breeze against her bare legs.

She sighed deeply and closed her eyes. And finally admitted to herself that she was in love with the man. Realised that this was, perhaps, the first time that she had ever been in love with anyone. Because, as she now recognised, in Gareth Lacey she'd at last found her soulmate . . .

'Oh hell,' Davina groaned.

Gareth stirred, but didn't lift his head. He didn't want to ask her what she meant. He was frightened she might tell him.

* * *

That night, Davina skulked in the shadows in the entrance hall in Wolsey, waiting for him to leave Walton for Hall.

She'd changed into black silk trousers and a mandarin-style black shirt, and the moment he was gone she slipped across the lawn and pushed open the door to Walton. Everything was quiet and remained so as she made her way to his rooms. His door was unlocked again, as most of them were, and her lips twisted. The big bad world outside of St Bede's couldn't reach anyone in here, could it? Except, of course, that it could, she thought, viciously sad, as she walked across the worn carpet to his desk. She found the key again, unlocked the bottom drawer and drew out the folder marked *Exam Papers*. She saw a dark blue spot appear on the pale blue folder, and for a moment stared at it stupidly. Then another spot appeared, and she suddenly realised that she was crying. The absorbent paper was soaking up her salty tears, expanding them slowly in an ever-increasing circle.

She angrily brushed the tears away, got up, and walked on leaden legs to the door, her prize clutched in her hand. No one saw her enter the library or go into the small photo-copying room off the main loggia.

'See, Gareth,' she murmured, as she carefully photocopied the exam papers for King Canute College's summer exam finals. 'Fate just isn't on your side.' She watched, half-hypnotised, as the bar of white light moved across the papers, making copies of the multiple-choice questions. Within just a few short minutes, she'd returned the papers to his room and was on her way back to Hall, the photocopies inside her bag.

She was acutely aware of the war being waged within her, the battle lines so clearly drawn. Her heart, which belonged to Gareth, had surprising strength. Her head, which belonged to David and the promise given to him on the day of his funeral, was cold and clear. And her soul, which would always be her own, but was now inexorably linked to Gareth's, was ominously silent.

Which one was going to win?

As she entered Hall and made her way to High Table, where Gareth waited for her, she realised that she had no idea.

And it scared her.

For the first time in her life, something scared her.

THIRTEEN

Alicia watched the familiar scenery of Warwickshire flash past the car window and glanced curiously across at her companion. Rupert was a very attractive man. Most women must find his combination of blond good looks, money and title an irresistible combination. And she wondered, idly, why it did so little for her. The answer came to her almost immediately: Jared, of course.

She gave a mental shrug, telling herself not to get maudlin. Or nervous. She was only going to a weekend house party and ball, after all, and was hardly a novice at such social events.

'Tired?' Rupert asked, taking his hand off the steering wheel long enough to give her fingers a tender squeeze.

Alicia smiled and shook her head. 'Just a bit weary, that's all. I haven't been sleeping well. The excitement of the play, I expect,' she lied glibly. For it wasn't the final, hectic preparations of the play that were wearing her out.

It was Jared. Ever since that party in the SCR last week she'd known something had gone horribly wrong. The teasing was gone. The togetherness was missing. The feeling of easy fondness overlaid by something deeper seemed to have disintegrated. He hadn't mentioned his plans for the future. Hadn't asked her out. Hadn't escorted her over to Hall.

And, try as she might to avoid thinking about it, she knew there could only be one explanation for all that. Neville hadn't been lying about the money. He really had paid him off.

Oh hell. She was going to cry! She looked hastily out of the window of the luxurious Rover and blinked back the hot, angry, disappointed tears that threatened to flood her lovely blue eyes. She took a deep breath. Pull yourself together girl, damn it. You're no longer a child who can cry like a baby when things don't go your way.

Rupert glanced across at her, studying her peach-perfect profile. 'Bored?' he murmured. 'I hate the tedious business of travelling too. But we'll be there soon, and believe me, there's nothing boring about Warrington.'

Alicia flashed him a quick smile. 'I'm sure there isn't,' she assured him, hearing plainly the deep pride in his voice. 'It was really nice of you to ask me, Rupert,' she said softly. After all, it wouldn't be fair to take out her own misery on Rupert. She turned back to the window, missing the look of joy which flared across Rupert's face.

Alicia knew she had to face facts. She wasn't the first woman to fall in love with the wrong man. Except Jared wasn't the wrong man, a stubborn voice suddenly piped up, so firmly that it made her jump. OK, so Jared was the right man for her. But where did that leave her? Oh, she could easily forgive him for taking money from her brother. What did mere money matter to her? But could she ever forgive him for leaving her to another man. Even one as harmless as Rupert?

That was harder. Much harder.

When she got back to Oxford, she'd just have to have it all out with him. Her heart leapt. Oh, very brave, Alicia, she thought mockingly. But what if he says he'd rather have the money than you. What will you do then?

'Here we are,' Rupert said, and she realised that they'd left the main roads some time before, and now were just turning off a leafy lane on to a private road.

126

'Look through the trees there . . .' Rupert slowed the car to point, and, sure enough, through the frothing greenness, Alicia caught a glimpse of golden turrets. 'Warrington,' Rupert breathed, with utter and evident satisfaction, as they turned a bend in the road and suddenly there was the house.

And it was some house. Built in the early 1700s, it had the classic elegance of the period. 'It's . . . magnificent!' Alicia breathed, overwhelmed, as anyone would be, by one of the more beautiful stately homes of England.

'Isn't it,' Rupert breathed. 'And it's mine. Or rather, it's my father's, at the moment. But it will be mine.'

When the bastard was dead.

'You're the oldest son?' she asked, realising, perhaps for the first time, the true lofty status of the man sitting next to her.

'The only son,' Rupert corrected her quickly. 'So all the land comes with the entailment too.' But not necessarily the family money, he thought grimly. This petty threat of his father's to leave his fortune to Rupert's sister was something that must never be allowed to happen. 'So,' he took a deep breath as he looked across at Alicia. 'What do you think? Could you see yourself living here?' he asked, in utter seriousness.

Alicia smiled. 'Oh yes! Dressed in a crinoline and carrying a lace parasol!'

Rupert didn't hear the lightness of her tone. Was deaf to the fact that she wasn't serious. Instead, he thought how wonderful she really would look in a crinoline. With her mass of raven hair, and those huge blue eyes, she would be perfect. Just like one of those portraits of his ancestors which lined the Great Hall. A famous beauty of her day.

Rupert came round and opened the door for her, his eyes running over her in approval. She was dressed in a designer suit and a matching blue blouse. The colour did wonders for her hair, which was swept back in a very elegant French pleat, and made her eyes simply . . . incredible. A floaty silvery-blue scarf of the very finest, sheerest silk billowed around her neck in the merest breeze, and this vision was the first thing Rupert's father saw as he walked down the fan-shaped front steps when he came to greet them.

Rupert, who'd seen him open the door and step out, felt his heart thump. It couldn't have been better.

'So, you've arrived at last,' a gruff voice spoke from just behind her. 'I thought you'd got . . . lost.'

The Earl of Warrington's eyes widened as Alicia spun around, her startled blue eyes wide with surprise.

'Father,' Rupert said, his voice cold.

The Earl of Warrington didn't appear to hear his son's greeting. In fact, he was still staring at Alicia and she felt herself blushing.

The Earl smiled, suddenly. It had been some time since he'd seen a lady blush, and once again, Rupert felt himself swell with pride. He, who knew his father so well, knew that Alicia was having just the effect on him that he'd been hoping she would. Even that blush was tailor-made to charm the old man.

'Father, this is Alicia Norman,' he introduced them briefly. 'Alicia, this is my father, the Earl of Warrington.'

Alicia fought back the absurd desire to curtsy. Instead she stepped forward and held out one long, pale, sensitive hand.

'I'm simply charmed,' the Earl murmured. 'Norman? Are you, by any chance, related to our literary-minded neighbours?'

Alicia smiled. 'Yes. My father owns—'

'I read it every week,' the Earl interrupted. 'Well, this is an unexpected bonus,' he said, giving his son a long, level look. The boy, at last, had done something right. His past dates for the ball had been something of a disaster.

He turned and walked her towards the house. Alicia, feeling slightly sorry for Rupert, turned and glanced over her shoulder at him. But far from looking put out at having his guest monopolised, he was beaming with obvious pleasure.

Alicia felt her heart constrict in fear and pity. Pity, because pleasing his austere and, she instinctively felt, largely unloving father meant so much to him. And fear, because she finally realised how much Rupert was relying on her to play the role of 'acceptable girlfriend'. She felt a frisson of foreboding snake down her spine as she stepped into the awe-inspiring hall.

This weekend suddenly had the feel of an endurance test.

* * *

Twenty-four hours later, Alicia stepped from her bath, wrapped herself in a huge fluffy white towel and stepped back into her bedroom, with its Queen Anne four-poster bed, rich pink silk hangings, and an original Turner on the far wall.

It was like something from a fantasy.

After their arrival, Rupert had informed her that dinner was at eight, in a small, cosy dining room just off the main hall. It had been, she was relieved to discover, a simple, family-only meal.

The Countess of Warrington was a very impressive lady, but as coldly polite and distant as an ice sculpture. As well as the Earl and Countess, Rupert's sister, Lady Camilla, and her fiancé had joined them for the evening. Camilla was like her brother in looks, but there all similarity ended. Where Rupert was self-effacing, Camilla was outgoing. While Rupert was sweet-natured, Camilla was astringent. Alicia was puzzled by the rather amused, speculative looks that she'd caught Lady Camilla cast her way all through dinner.

All in all, Alicia had been glad when the meal was over.

Now she sighed as she turned the setting on her hairdryer to a cooler temperature, affixed the brush and began to dry her hair.

She'd spent a lovely day, riding in the water-meadows with Rupert, enjoying a pub lunch, before returning to the house. There, she'd played a game of chess with her host, narrowly losing. Rupert, she'd noticed again, had beamed with happiness as she scored yet another hit with his father.

All in all, she thought now, her stay at Warrington hadn't quite been the ordeal she'd been expecting.

Throughout the afternoon, caterers had arrived by the van load. Masses of flowers had been carried in. The housekeeper and an army of chattering servants had busily prepared for tonight's ball.

Her hair now dry and framing her face in a mass of black waves, Alicia decided to be daring and leave it down for a change.

She applied the barest hint of make-up — just a touch of gold eyeshadow and a natural-coloured glossy lipstick — and donned the silk and lace knickers she'd brought with her and the wired, uplifting bra that was so uncomfortable to wear, but which gave such good results. She unrolled her stockings, putting them on with infinite care, and walked to the wardrobe to retrieve the ballgown she'd brought with her.

She pulled the gown out and ran a hand over the pink silk. It was a bold gown, one that she and her mother had chosen together on one of their trips to Milan. As she put it on and glanced in the mirror, she was relieved to see it was as spectacular as she remembered it. It left her shoulders completely bare, and the contrast of her creamy skin and raven locks against the deep pink strapless top which covered her breasts was breath-taking. Her uplift bra gave her a modest but most definitely appealing cleavage. Below the stiff bodice, the gown nipped into a tight waist, and fell in an almost dead straight, lustrously gleaming line to her ankles. She slipped her feet into a pair of silver satin heels, donned long white gloves and looped an unusual necklace of jet and silver, bought to go with the dress, around her neck so that it sparkled and glowed at her throat. When she stepped back to view herself, she knew that she would not let Rupert down.

The sound of cars arriving outside had her grabbing her tiny, envelope-style evening purse and moving to the door.

Rupert was hovering in the corridor, waiting for her. He looked perfect in his black tuxedo, and the way he stopped dead and gaped at her as she walked towards him made her heart swell in tender fondness. 'Rupert,' she said softly, and held out her arm. 'Will you escort me downstairs?'

The hall was full of people as they turned the bend in the sweeping staircase. Winston, the butler, was just admitting an older couple. A mammoth urn of white orchids, freesias, roses and carnations frothed in the centre of the black-and-white-tiled hall.

It was one of those magical experiences when everyone seemed to freeze in a never-to-be-forgotten moment of time. The older couple looked up at the spectacularly handsome, contrasting young couple coming down the stairs, and their faces softened.

The Earl and Countess followed their gaze.

The Countess, for the first time ever, looked approving. By her side, Alicia felt Rupert swell. The evening was already a success. And she was glad. But she was even more pleased that tomorrow she'd be going back to Oxford.

Back to Jared.

The Warrington Ball passed as the March Ball always had — in a whirl of vintage champagne, dancing, gourmet food and fine music.

Rupert danced with Alicia constantly, and the fact was not missed by the more matrimony-minded ladies of the county. Midnight came and went. Two o'clock came and went. Eventually Warrington began to empty, and Alicia bade the Earl and Countess goodnight.

By four o'clock, the house was silent.

Feeling bone-weary, Alicia crawled into bed and fell instantly asleep. She was awoken by the sound of blackbirds singing and a heavy object landing on the end of her bed. She opened bleary eyes, saw a descending blond head, and felt herself being kissed. She struggled instantly into alert, appalled wakefulness.

'Rupert,' she spluttered, pushing him away from her. He was still dressed in his tuxedo, and when he leaned back from her, his face was oddly flushed. She realised she wasn't the only one who had drunk too much champagne.

'Rupert,' she said again, sitting up against the headboard and pulling the sheets up under her chin. 'I don't think you should be here,' she warned.

Uneasily, she realised she was potentially in a very embarrassing position. On the other hand, she didn't intend to put up with any nonsense from Rupert, either.

'Sorry,' he said quietly, instantly putting her fears to rest. 'I know I shouldn't have. But you looked so beautiful, lying there asleep. I really came in to give you this.'

And, while she wilted in relief, he suddenly held out his hand. In it was the most amazing ring she'd ever seen. A square-cut sapphire surrounded by a starburst of diamonds. A veritable queen's ransom of a ring.

It looked ancient. And priceless.

She gaped at it. 'Rupert?' she breathed. 'What . . .'

'It's the Warrington ring,' he said simply. 'It's an heirloom. It's been in the family for over a hundred years.'

Alicia felt her mouth fall open. She wondered, for one brief moment, if she was actually dreaming. If she'd never woken up. 'But . . . we're not engaged,' she blurted out. She pushed the hair out of her eyes. Tried to struggle free from this feeling of growing unreality. Had she missed something somewhere? Had she . . .

'I wanted to make it official, darling,' Rupert said, leaning suddenly closer. And for the first time, Alicia clearly saw, in the gleaming, feverish light of his eyes, the ugly, scary, unmistakable glint of insanity.

She felt herself go cold. Deathly cold.

'I know Father approves of you,' Rupert carried on, his voice tumbling over itself now in its eagerness to explain. 'And that's important. Really important.' Once again, he reached out to grab her arm in a familiar gesture, but this time his fingers curled around her wrist in a strong, talon-like grip.

She licked her lips, blinking, trying to force herself to think. Keep him talking, she heard a quiet, firm voice pipe up in the back of her head. Whatever happens, keep him talking. 'Is it? Why?' she asked gently, as if she was talking to a terrified horse that might bolt at any moment.

'Because of the money, you see,' Rupert said, waving a hand in the air. 'He was going to give it all to Camilla, but now he's seen you, I know he won't.'

He's not making sense, Alicia thought in growing panic and hysteria. He's not making any kind of sense at all! She fought back a desperate wave of panic. Of self-recrimination. Why hadn't she spotted this . . . mental unbalance in him before? Was she so blind? So stupid? Sure, he'd had too much to drink, but this was way beyond that.

'I see. Money,' she echoed, trying to keep her voice flat and calm and soothing. She had to get him out of here. Then she would be able to think!

'But now it'll be fine,' Rupert rushed to assure her. He didn't like to see his beloved so upset. 'Father approves of you. We'll be married, and you'll have sons to carry on the family name. That will please him.'

'Yes,' Alicia murmured faintly. 'I'm sure it will. But, Rupert, don't you think you should leave now? If your father were to catch us together like this, he might . . . er . . .'

'Oh, yes, of course, darling,' he agreed. 'You're so sweet. So old-fashioned. But you're right of course. It simply wouldn't do.' He was so relieved it was all over. She'd accepted him. They were engaged. He was safe.

Alicia let out a shaky breath. Then, before she could stop him, he suddenly grabbed her hand. She felt her whole body stiffen in shock, but he only reached for the ring and slipped it on her finger. To her horror it was a tight fit. She felt herself wince as he forced it brutally over her knuckle. In portraits of more recent Warrington women, she'd noticed this very ring adorning their little fingers.

But Rupert had pushed it on to her engagement finger. She could feel the finger throbbing slightly at the tight restriction of the band.

'Now, I'd really better leave,' Rupert said. 'I can't resist you!' Then, with a smile of dazzling brilliance that in itself could never be classed as normal, he leaned forward and kissed her again.

Alicia had never in her life been prepared for something like this, and simply froze. But the kiss was soon over, and then he was backing away, smiling, talking inanely about life at Warrington, about looking in the attics to see if he could find a crinoline and lace gown for her to wear for their wedding, and she could think of nothing to do but watch him retreat. Then he was gone.

Instantly, Alicia shot out of bed and locked the door.

She leaned against it panting. She was scared. And upset.

She'd never had to deal with anyone with such delusions before.

She thought about the cold natures of the Earl and Countess, and shook her head. It was not surprising, really, that a man as sensitive and vulnerable as Rupert should have problems.

But . . . Oh, what should she do about it?

She ran to the bathroom and thrust her hand under the tap, rubbed soap vigorously around the ring, but it was no good. She simply couldn't get it off. And, in truth, she was wary about pulling too hard, in case she should damage the ring. It was obviously a museum-quality piece. She forced herself to take a deep breath. Stood over the sink, gasping and shaking and telling herself uselessly not to panic.

Her finger was swollen, that was all. Rupert had bruised it putting the ring on. As soon as the swelling went down, she would take the ring off, and send it back to the Earl with a note of explanation. But even as she thought it, she shook her head. How could you write a letter to an earl telling him his son needed psychiatric help? What would he do to Rupert? She shuddered, imagining his rage at his son. Would Rupert be locked away in an institution?

No. Surely not. She shuddered again. Not even the Earl would be so cruel. Would he?

She endured a miserable few hours then, spent pacing her room and waiting for the rest of the household to stir.

After such a late night, they were not going to be early risers. She packed, longing to get away. She even contemplated calling for a taxi, and leaving like a thief in the night. But somehow, she couldn't do that to Rupert. It would be so cowardly. So unfair to leave him to face the music alone. No matter how badly he'd scared her, she was sure he wouldn't harm her, and she didn't have the heart to do that.

So she waited until the breakfast gong sounded, and then, dressed once more in her blue suit, went down to the small breakfast room. But there, the Countess noticed the ring almost at once. Camilla, in the process of helping herself to bacon and eggs, froze at her mother's gasp. The Earl noticed the frantic head-bobbing motion of his wife as she kept looking pointedly at Alicia's hand.

Instinctively, as Alicia walked towards the table, she tried to keep her hand behind her back to hide it, but suddenly Rupert was there. Taking her hand firmly in his own. Leading her to the table where everyone could see his mark of ownership.

And Alicia didn't dare say anything, realising grimly that she was no psychologist. She might do Rupert irreparable mental harm if she just blurted out that it was all a mistake. That she didn't love him. That she had no intention of marrying him. What she had to do, she realised, was get him to see a psychiatrist. Perhaps once they were back in Oxford, away from this damned house and these awful people, she could persuade him to see someone.

The Earl glanced at the ring. Looked quickly up at his beaming son, then thoughtfully at Alicia.

'Well,' he said quietly, as Alicia felt her heart sink to her shoes. 'We have reason to celebrate, it seems?'

FOURTEEN

Davina walked up the now familiar Banbury streets, and made her way to a burger joint in the shadow of an impressive church. Sitting in the far corner, furthest away from the counter, was Gavin Brock. She was all business as she dropped a rather battered satchel beside her chair.

'I've deposited the money in your bank,' she told him abruptly. 'You can check if you like.'

Gavin did just that, walking to the nearest public telephone box, where a very helpful voice on the other end cheerfully informed him that his bank account was now looking very healthy indeed.

'Well?' she asked abruptly, as Gavin returned.

'Everything seems OK,' he admitted grudgingly. Then he leaned back cockily in the chair, and said more firmly, 'Yeah. All right, let's do it. What's the next step?'

She felt her throat constrict, and realised, too late, that she'd been hoping he'd back down. But now there was nothing stopping her. The destruction of Gareth Lacey could go ahead.

Gareth! She swallowed the anguished cry, and took a deep breath. But the unspoken cry seemed to echo around the inside of her skull, like a trapped banshee. Grimly, she reached for the satchel and extracted a slim folder.

'Those — the . . . er . . . things?' he asked nervously. 'Can I have a look?'

Davina's lips twisted. 'That was the general idea, yes,' she said and watched him glance through the Modern Poetry exam papers.

'These multiple-choice questions are killers,' he whistled. 'I'd have been guessing at least half of them, if not more. OK. So what's the next step?'

'The next step is to have one of your tutors accidentally find these papers in your possession,' Davina said crisply.

Gavin grimaced. 'And how are we going to arrange that? They don't go around rifling your pockets or demanding that you show them your books.'

Davina nodded. 'I know. So, how are we going to do it?' she mused, drumming her fingers on the table. For a while they were both silent. Eventually Davina sighed. 'Well, there's no way we can be subtle about it,' she said at last. 'You do have to hand in essays every now and then, don't you?' she asked Gavin sharply.

'Yeah. Usually to that new bloke, Mr Carter.'

'Right. So, when you hand in your next essay, slip one of the question pages into it — only one, mind. Then, when he takes you aside and asks you what it is, you can act scared and defiant. Tell him the paper must have got caught up in your essay by mistake. Try to grab it back. He'll question you, and you, very reluctantly, tell him that you paid good money for those papers. That Modern Poetry is your weakest subject and you knew you needed a little extra help if you were to pass the exams. Tell him that you heard on the grapevine that Gareth Lacey could be paid for advance copies of his papers. That he'd done it before. So you contacted him, and he told you it was a thousand pounds a paper. You paid it.'

'Right,' Gavin grinned. 'Mr Carter's still wet behind the ears, and this is his first teaching post, so he's bound to fall for it. Funnily enough, I think he got his degree at Oxford. Yeah, don't worry. I can handle Mr Carter all right.'

Davina nodded. 'Right. So you'll do it this week, yes?'

'I can do it tomorrow. I've got an essay due about Ted Hughes and some pike.'

Davina winced and pushed away from the table. 'Well then. That's all settled,' she said. But couldn't quite convince herself of that. She walked to the door, and out into the wet and windy day. It *was* settled. She was about to achieve what she'd come to Oxford for. Justice for David, and revenge for herself. She walked back to the railway station, and on the way to Oxford took out her notebook and composed a short poem about the glories of revenge right there on the train. It flowed out of her like molten lead, heavy, ponderous, deeply human. It was one of those rare moments when a poem wrote itself. Except, when she'd finished it, it wasn't glorious at all. It was sad. And empty.

And she knew it was going to be one of her finest poems.

* * *

In his room, Gareth Lacey saw the attractive blonde student to the door. 'And remember, Leigh Hunt and Keats need to be explored together. Take them separately, and you don't get half the sense of power in their work.'

The blonde nodded enthusiastically as Gareth gently shut the door behind her, ignoring the interested look in her eyes.

He walked to his table and gathered his papers together, wondering if he could push the girl to a first. At the moment she was strictly 2.1. But with some effort . . . He put her file away in the cabinet, and as he did so, the file of another student caught his eye. The tag on the side was black, indicating that the student was deceased.

Slowly, reluctantly, he pulled it out. David Garrett.

Just the sight of the boy's name made everything inside him wince. He hesitated, his hand hovering over the innocuous beige folder. He should just leave it. Should just close the drawer shut, and then get on with something else. Life had to go on.

Last term he'd had this beige file out time and time again, torturing himself with it. Asking himself over and over if he'd done the right thing. If he shouldn't have spoken out . . . He sighed and lifted the folder clear of the cabinet drawer, walking with it to the big leather armchair set by the log fire blazing away in the hearth. He sat down and reached for the tortoiseshell glasses lying on the table, slipping them on and opening the folder, already knowing its contents by heart.

The first page was the usual form containing the student's personal details. After that, end-of-term reports. His prelim exam results. Then . . . the mass of paperwork that dealt with his cheating.

Then his notification of expulsion. Then the stark announcement of his death. Gareth had clipped out his obituary notice from the local Hastings paper that he'd asked the librarian to get for him. No need for it, of course, but by then . . . by then, Gareth thought, he was feeling as guilty as sin. Because he should have known there was something wrong with the boy. Hell, it was obvious for anyone who was looking. The trouble was . . . he hadn't been looking.

Gareth leaned back in his chair, slipping off the glasses, his eyes filling with tears he could no longer shed. When David had first come up, he'd been a typical first-year student. Bright, but not brilliant. Open, refreshingly honest, with a cheeky sense of humour that had instantly endeared him to everyone, Gareth included. And then he'd begun to change . . . to get moody. Paranoid. Angry.

Gareth sat up in the chair, pushing the glasses back on his face. He should have known something was badly wrong. Instead he'd put it down to teenage angst and the Oxford blues. And he'd just blithely assumed that David would eventually settle, that whatever was bothering the lad would sort itself out. And therein lay the guilt. The awful sense of failing the boy. All that pain he must have been going through . . .

Grimly, with a sense of dread, Gareth turned to the very last page of the file. To the letter that he had shown no one, not even Sin-Jun. The letter that he had kept back even from the coroner.

The letter David had written him as he started to succumb to the massive dose of sleeping pills he'd taken . . .

Gareth read it again, although it was already committed to memory. For ever burned into his brain. And, once he'd read it — yet again — he shut the folder, put it back in the filing cabinet and locked it. And then he reached for the typewriter and the final chapter of his latest book on the life and times of Alfred Lord Tennyson.

But the ghost of David stayed with him, long into the darkening evening.

* * *

Alicia walked into the noisy theatre, still feeling as if the weight of the whole world was on her shoulders.

The ride back from Warrington had been a nightmare. Rupert had been effervescent, talking without stopping; about what a hit she'd been with the family, about how happy she'd made him, about their wonderful future together. It was as if he didn't dare pause for breath, and she'd had to sit and listen to it, with a growing sense of horror and helplessness, fighting back the urge to scream.

It had been a huge relief to get back to St Bede's yesterday afternoon. To finally be able to say goodbye to him. To finally drag herself to her room and the blessed peace and quiet and sanctuary of it. But last night, as she'd lain in bed, sleepless and heart-sick, her mind had just gone round in ever widening circles. All night long she'd tossed and turned, going over her options. The Warrington ring still throbbing on her hand, too tight to remove.

She'd thought about going to the principal, but something about telling Sin-Jun of Rupert made her uneasy. Wouldn't he be more inclined to believe that it was she who was being hysterical, not Rupert? No, somehow, rightly or wrongly, Alicia didn't trust Sin-Jun.

She was sorely tempted to go to Dr Lacey with it all. She felt instinctively that Gareth Lacey would believe her, or at the very least listen to her. But that morning she'd risen, huge shadows beneath her eyes, having come to the conclusion that it simply wasn't fair for her to talk to anyone else until she'd had a chance to talk to Rupert.

She was a grown woman now. She owed it to herself to think things through very carefully before she acted. And surely, by now, Rupert must have wound down enough for her to speak to him rationally? After all, she and everyone else had assumed him to be a functioning human being all this time. His mental illness surely couldn't be all that advanced that he wouldn't listen to reason.

She was so woefully ignorant about things like this. Suddenly Alicia felt too young to cope with it all. But it was Rupert, poor Rupert, who was the one in real trouble.

She'd tried again to remove the Warrington ring with soap, but the damned thing seemed to be possessed. She simply couldn't get it over her knuckle. Now, as she walked into the theatre and listened with a lurching heart to Jared's voice as he cajoled Emily into a more understated performance, the ring throbbed on her hand, a ghastly reminder of her predicament. She needed to speak to Jared, of course. She realised that the moment she heard his voice again.

She hurried down the aisle, dumping her bag and coat on the seat and walking forward, eager to get back into his orbit. To feel his presence beside her. To touch him, if only in passing . . .

'Ah, here's the sleeping beauty at last,' Emily grinned from the stage. 'Author, tell this buffoon that the murder victim has a right to go over the top.'

Alicia smiled at her friend, wanting to kiss her. Emily was so . . . normal. Such a breath of reality. So uncomplicated. 'You clown,' she laughed. 'You know full well you've got our tragic heroine down pat by now.'

Today was 1 April, the day before the play was to be shown, and nerves were running high. Jared ran a harassed hand through his hair and looked at Alicia. He knew he'd have to do it eventually, so he might as well get it over with.

He'd just endured the longest weekend of his life.

When Rupert had invited her home during the party in the SCR, he'd been torn between the desire to march up to them and tell Rupert where to stick his party, while another part of him, a more treacherous, unsure, feeble part of him, had insisted that Alicia deserved fancy parties in big glamorous houses. That she'd been raised in that environment, and that he'd been dreaming when he thought that she could be happy in a totally different world. His world.

And so he'd stood, rooted to the spot, too cowardly to act, but all the time willing her to say no. Silently sending out telepathic messages, begging her to turn him down.

But she hadn't, of course. Why should she?

And when he'd seen the look of triumph in her brother's eyes Jared had felt sick. When he'd seen the flare of relief that so clearly stated that the other man had won, and he, the upstart, had lost, he'd wanted to smash something. And it had hurt him. Stupid, he knew. But then, he'd been stupid all along to think that he was good enough for her. To believe that their romance had ever stood a chance.

So he'd spent the weekend forcing himself to come to terms with it. Nights spent tossing and turning, imagining her dancing in Rupert's arms. Days spent telling himself that love was just a fantasy worth having, but not a reality that was ever going to be his. At least, not with Alicia Norman.

But now, standing beside her again . . . the fantasy was back. Stronger than the reality. Like a beautiful weed, determined to grow, no matter what. 'So, how was the ball?' he heard himself ask cheerfully. The others also crowded around, eager to hear the details, and Alicia did her best to relay them.

'But that's enough of that,' she finally managed to fend off their curiosity. 'How's the dress rehearsal going?'

Taking the hint, the cheerful cast began to disperse back to their marks on the stage. But before Jared could turn away, she reached out and grabbed his arm. 'Jared,' she said urgently. 'I need to speak to you. Something's happened.'

Being so close to her now, he could see the dark shadows beneath her eyes. The tense line to her mouth. He felt himself stiffen. 'What's wrong?'

But before she could speak, the others on the stage gave a sudden roar of ribbing and mock-handclapping, and they all turned to watch Rupert jogging down the aisle towards them.

'Sorry I'm late,' he called breathlessly. 'I overslept.'

'Who with!' one of the wags, who was busy setting up the scenery, shot back drolly. Catcalls and whistles followed.

Jared, who was still standing next to her, saw the way Alicia paled. 'Alicia,' he hissed, his voice sharp. 'Alicia! What's the matter?'

Rupert's head slowly turned their way. For one instant, his eyes narrowed on them, then he smiled, walking forward. 'Darling,' he said, in a clear, loud, ringing voice as he made his way towards her, hands outstretched.

Alicia couldn't help herself. She took a step back. One part of her knew she was being hideously unfair and immature. The other part screamed at her that this man needed help, not neglect. She must persuade him to see a psychiatrist. She simply must make him seek help. She cringed at the thought of going to see a psychiatrist on her own, and coming out with that old chestnut, 'Doctor, I have this friend who needs help . . .' No. She had to make Rupert see for himself that he needed help. She would be there for him. All the way. And she wasn't going to do that by backing away from him whenever he came near. So she forced herself to take a step towards him. To smile. To look pleased to see him.

But Jared had noticed her instinctive withdrawal. Had noticed the strange play of emotions cross her face. And he felt a deep rock of dread build in his stomach. What the hell was going on? What had happened at this damned ball? What had she wanted to tell him?

'Rupert,' Alicia said, as brightly as she could manage. 'I'm glad you're here. We need to talk . . .' She wanted to get him out of there. Away from those watching, curious eyes. She reached for his arm, trying to tug him in the direction of the exit.

But Rupert wasn't budging. 'Of course, darling,' he agreed, then patted her hand and turned her to face the stage. 'Have you told them all our news yet?'

Alicia jerked under his arm. 'No! Rupert, I think we should wait,' she babbled quickly.

'Oh, don't be shy, darling,' he admonished her tenderly. 'I want the whole world to know. Listen, you lot,' he called cheerfully across the stage, as the cast began to shuffle forward, sensing something of interest. 'I've got great news. This weekend I asked Alicia to marry me. And she's agreed.'

There was dead silence for the merest heartbeat.

Alicia felt the world move away from her for an instant, and then come rushing back in a wave of sound and commotion.

The cast on the stage, after an initial surprised second, began to jump down and surround them, slapping Rupert on the back and congratulating them. Only Emily stayed on the stage, staring at her friend, dumbstruck.

Alicia blinked, trying to smile at the women who were gathered around her, chattering excitedly. The girl who was to play the victim's mother suddenly spotted her engagement ring and shrieked. 'Hell's bells! Look at that!' She grabbed Alicia's hand to display the impressive Warrington ring to everyone.

Alicia's hand had gone numb. Like the rest of her. Over Rupert's blond head, her eyes searched for Jared. He was standing just where she'd left him.

Looking at her as if she'd just shot him with a revolver.

FIFTEEN

Alicia went through the gate where Rupert, living out in his second year, had his flat. She pushed the door open timidly and found, beside the staircase, a list of names and addresses which told her that Rupert Greyling-Simms had one of the more spacious flats on the second floor.

After Rupert's stark announcement at rehearsals that morning, she'd found it impossible to talk to Jared alone, and Rupert had never left her side. It was only after they broke for the morning that she was able to persuade Rupert to leave, and only then by agreeing to have a late lunch with him.

But Jared had been so busy with last-minute hitches that, with the time ticking on, Alicia had had to leave without speaking to him.

Rupert, who'd been standing by his window for the last half hour keeping a look out for her, quickly opened the door. She followed him into a pleasant sitting-room, where a small round table beneath the big bay window had been set with plates of glamorous food and an open bottle of champagne. It was French, a vintage year.

She took her seat nervously as he served her. At last he sat down opposite her, raising his glass. 'To us,' he said.

And Alicia suddenly knew it was now or never. 'Rupert,' she said softly, her gentle heart already breaking for him, 'there is *no* us. I tried to tell you so at Warrington but . . .'

Rupert shook his head. 'Don't be silly, Alicia,' his voice was just a touch sharp. 'We were made for each other. Everyone thinks so. My father. Your brother. It's perfect.'

Alicia slowly lowered her glass on to the table and sighed. 'Rupert, I don't think we make a perfect match.' She emphasized the word 'I' just enough so that he couldn't possibly misunderstand. 'I hardly know you, after all! And, if you're honest,' she added, choosing her words very carefully now, 'you must admit to yourself that you don't love me . . .'

'But I do!'

'We've hardly talked . . .'

'But all that time spent in the theatre . . .'

'All that time in the theatre we talked about the play, Rupert,' she said softly.

Rupert flushed. He could feel an awful yawning gap opening up around him. She was going to leave him! He was going to be alone, with his father's scorn and his mother's disappointment, and Camilla sneering at him . . . He went so pale Alicia almost cried out loud. She was hurting him!

She, who wouldn't even voluntarily swat a wasp. 'Rupert!' she cried, reaching for his hand, pulling it into her own. 'Rupert, I want you to agree to come and see someone with me,' she began, and then stopped as she saw his eyes flicker.

'See someone?' he almost whispered. Images from his childhood flashed hideously across his mind. Hadn't his nanny said something just like that to his mother once? When he'd been seven. Or was it eight? See someone.

'You mean a psychiatrist, don't you?' Rupert said flatly. He shook his head. 'No,' he said firmly. 'No, never again.'

Alicia felt a jolt of alarm shoot through her. 'Again? You mean . . . Rupert, have you seen a therapist before?'

He turned his face away, but he was remembering being driven to Quiet Acres, the small residential home in the Lake District. His father had told everyone he was going away to

146

school. No one was to know that the Earl of Warrington's son had 'difficulties'. Oh no. No one must ever even suspect that . . . Rupert's face twisted as he fought back the desire to cry. His hands clenched around his champagne glass. 'No,' he said again, his voice high and wavering, almost falsetto in its cadence now. He shook his head. 'No, I'm not going back there . . .' He was on the verge of hysteria.

Alicia had no idea what he was talking about. She was only aware of a growing sense of horror as the young and handsome man, who seemed to have it all, began to disintegrate in front of her eyes.

'Rupert,' she whispered, appalled, ashamed, afraid for him. 'Rupert, it's all right . . .'

'I need you, Alicia. You're the only one who can save me,' he pleaded. 'I have to marry you. I have to!' The delicate stem of the glass he was holding snapped in half, nicking his finger. He threw it down, and a slow, red trickle of blood began to seep down his hand.

Alicia got to her feet, a cold river snaking down her back as she wondered if there was anyone in the house besides themselves. Wondered if anyone would hear her if she screamed. She took a deep breath. 'All right, Rupert,' she said softly, as soothingly as she could. It was not easy when her voice was shaking as badly as the rest of her. 'We'll talk about this again after the play.'

Rupert smiled suddenly. 'It's a wonderful play, Alicia. I'll be good in it, I promise.' His voice was almost childlike now in its heart-rending desire to please. 'I'll be good — just for you.'

Alicia blinked, stunned by the sudden change in his face. In his voice. In his character. She licked her dry lips. 'I know you will. I have to get back now to see that everything is all right. It's the opening night tomorrow, remember?' She began edging towards the door, and he moved suddenly, his face beaming.

'Of course,' he walked up to her and hugged her exuberantly. 'Once all that's over, we can concentrate on us, right?'

Alicia, who'd frozen in terror as he'd swept her into his arms, managed to nod. She pulled free, moved to the door, stuttered goodbye and all but ran into the street. Her heart was racing.

One thing was now sure. She would have to talk to the Earl of Warrington. He must be told about Rupert's . . . relapse.

When she got back to her room in St Bede's, she attacked the ring on her finger with ferocious force. Even if she had to break her finger, she was going to remove the ring before the night was over.

* * *

Davina climbed out of the seat of the self-drive removal van Gareth had hired and jumped lithely on to the rain-washed path. For the next few hours they worked together with quiet concentration as they got the furniture settled into the cottage.

'Let's break for tea, shall we?' he said, as the clock he'd hung carefully on the wall five minutes ago showed him it was nearing four o'clock.

'Wherever I may roam, all of civilised England still stops at four o'clock for tea and crumpets,' she mocked.

'Don't knock it,' Gareth growled at her, leaning his dusty arms across the top of one of the shelves as he got his breath back. 'I've got a thermos in the van.' He retrieved it and set up the tea things. Something about the sight of him, sitting at the table in the middle of the cosy kitchen, made her heart contract. Perhaps it was because she'd never thought of any man, complete with hearth and home, as being her destiny. Or perhaps it was because she knew she would never see him like this again. Relaxed. Happy. Innocent. Whole.

Gareth raised his steaming beaker. 'To Spindlewood, and all who live in 'er,' he toasted.

Forcing back a wave of guilt that seemed to rock her, Davina accepted the mug. 'Why Spindlewood?' she asked, looking around her.

'Because of all the Spindlewood bushes that are growing wild in the jungle out there,' he nodded to the overgrown garden outside the kitchen window.

Solemnly she clinked her beaker against his. He was calling their cottage 'Spindlewood'. The thought was like the pang of an abscessed tooth. Because she knew she would never live here. The dream that had led him to buy and name this cottage was a dream that was as far beyond her reach as . . . as . . . living on the moon.

'It'll get dark early, the weather being so bad today,' she forced herself to change the subject, and glanced out at the dark lowering clouds that skulked across the sky. She simply couldn't tell him that she'd be leaving. Soon.

She'd woken that morning knowing that, for the first time in her life, there was something that she couldn't face. And that was being with him, as a trusted lover, when his world fell apart. Watching his face as he realised who had engineered it all . . .

Coward. A word she'd never thought would ever be applied to her. But his love had turned her into a coward. Ironic to think that, before he was even aware they were at war, he should win such a major victory and never even know it.

But then perhaps it was only poetic justice. Nemesis, the goddess of retribution, had an even-handed way of doling out her punishments. She would have to write a poem dedicated to her by way of a 'thank you for the lesson', Davina mused sadly.

She sighed deeply and rubbed the back of her neck.

She heard him get up and knew exactly what he was going to do. If she had any sense at all, she'd stop him. 'Mmm . . .' she murmured blissfully, as his fingers pushed her own aside and began to knead with surprising firmness and accuracy.

If only . . . If only she didn't love him.

If only she didn't hate him.

'Life gets complicated,' she said quietly.

She felt the fingers on her neck pause, then once again begin their firm, circular caresses. 'Oh?'

'I'm not moving in here,' Davina said flatly.

The fingers didn't hesitate.

'Why not?' Gareth said mildly.

'Because it's not a good idea. Believe me.'

Gareth looked down at the top of her spiky blonde head, feeling the smoothness of her flesh beneath his. Warm. Melting now, under the ministrations of his fingers. 'All right,' he said quietly. But he was not giving up.

Davina felt a trickle of something run down her spine. Not unease, exactly. But something . . . perhaps a warning. Something that told her never to underestimate this man. For all his gentleness, his sensitivity, his sophistication, she sensed a male power that, for all her experience of men, she'd never encountered before. She leaned back and looked up at him, her green eyes flashing like fire. 'You're up to something,' she said, more as a statement of fact than an accusation.

Gareth looked down at her. 'No,' he responded softly. 'Unless you call patience being up to something.'

Patience. Davina shivered. Yes. He had a lot of patience. And for all her own ferocity, for all her own passion, for all her own ruthlessness, she had the sudden premonition that, in the end, it was going to be Gareth's patience that undid her.

* * *

Jared glanced up as a knock sounded on his door.

'Come in,' he called, and shot to his feet as Alicia stepped inside and, with a curiously harassed look over her shoulder, quickly shut the door behind her.

Jared, who'd been puzzling over his bank statement, felt himself go hot, then cold. 'Alicia,' he said, trying to sound casual when all he really wanted to do was walk across the space between them and shake her. Demand to know what the hell she thought she was doing, breaking his heart as carelessly as she had.

He shook his head, knowing that he couldn't demand any such thing. He had no right to.

'Well, they say every cloud has a silver lining,' he forced himself to talk about something normal. 'The damned bank has made some mistake with my account. I dare say it's a computer blip. Either that, or somebody somewhere must be wondering where their ten grand has gone. I suppose I'll have to go down to the bank tomorrow and get it sorted.'

Alicia slowly began to smile. Of course, she understood at once what Neville had been playing at. 'Oh, Jared!' she cried, flinging herself across the room. All the strain of the last few days, plus the sheer relief of knowing that he hadn't been bought off, came tumbling out of her.

Jared just had time to turn, catch her, then stumble back against the edge of his bed as she launched herself into his arms. He felt himself falling backwards. The bedsprings creaked like an animal in pain as they landed, in a tangle of limbs, on the narrow mattress. He found himself flat on his back, Alicia on top of him. Crying. And laughing. And kissing him.

Jared froze, then melted. His arms came around her, holding her close, hardly able to believe those lips were real. That her small hands clinging on to his waist were actual flesh and blood. That the touch of her long hair against his face wasn't just a mirage.

'Alicia,' he murmured, cupping her sweet face in his hands, looking up into those sparkling brilliant blue eyes. 'What's going on, girl?' he said softly. 'And . . .' his voice and eyes sharpened, 'where's your ring?' For he'd noticed now that her hand was wonderfully, marvellously, miraculously bare of that damned Rock of Gibraltar.

'I finally managed to get it off,' Alicia said, still not sure whether to laugh, cry, or do both.

Sniffing a little, wearily she pushed a long lock of black hair back from her face and let the whole story pour out of her. First her brother's perfidy, because that was easier and less painful to explain. And then, as Jared grew slowly more pale and appalled, the story of what had really happened to her at Warrington. Rupert's dreadful family. The tale of the ring and how it had swollen her finger, making it impossible to get off. And, finally, her lunchtime meeting with Rupert. 'So you see,' she finally said quietly, her tear-stained cheeks pale, but her voice more composed now, 'it sounds as if he has a history of mental illness. And he won't agree to see a psychiatrist. I think he's terrified of them. And whenever I try to tell him that we're not engaged, he just won't listen to me. He keeps saying that he needs me. Oh, Jared, what am I going to do?'

Jared reached for one of her hands and slowly drew it to his lips. He kissed the centre of her palm tenderly. Then looked at her out of loving dark brown eyes. 'You mean,' he corrected her softly, 'what are *we* going to do?'

She smiled, a tremulous, exhausted, but radiant smile. 'Thank you,' she said softly. Simply.

Jared nodded. 'Well . . . we could talk to the new Experimental Psychology don. Or . . . who's Rupert's Moral Tutor, do you know?' Alicia didn't.

'We'll find out,' Jared said quietly. 'I wonder whether the Reverend Rex Jimson-Clarke could help . . .'

Alicia felt so much better. Not because Jared had an instant answer (who on earth would, given circumstances like these?), but because she now knew she was not alone. She felt safer. Comforted. She ran a hand lightly up Jared's chest, then felt a questing hardness rise up beneath her. She flushed, realising that Jared himself was blushing.

He made to move her off his lap, but Alicia dug her fingers into his arm. 'No!' she said quickly. 'I . . . I don't want to move.'

She leaned forward, undoing his shirt buttons. Jared's eyes widened. 'Alicia,' he said hoarsely. Warningly.

Alicia shook her head. 'No,' she said again, enigmatically. She dipped her head, running her tongue beneath the opening in his shirt, licking his warm, slightly salty skin.

Jared dragged in a ragged breath. 'Alicia,' he said again, more softly this time. 'Have you ever . . . ?'

'No,' Alicia said again, and smiled.

Jared groaned. 'Alicia,' he said again, his voice a mere croak this time. Alicia laughed, feeling giddy. She reached for his belt, undoing it and unzipping his jeans. She watched his wonderful eyes darken to midnight.

'I don't . . .' Jared began, but then she slipped her hand inside his jeans, and with the side of her knuckles began to gently but firmly rub him. His words were cut off with a sudden gasp. His eyelids drifted closed. He felt his arms come up to grab the old-fashioned bedhead behind him, his hands curling around the iron bars there in a tight, compulsive grip.

His body began to heat up, as if someone had turned on a sunlamp. Alicia got up, but only to slip out of her boots and panties. Through narrowed eyes, Jared watched her, knowing he should do something to stop her, but knowing, too, that he wasn't going to. She was wearing a warm jersey skirt, and when she climbed back over him, hitching it up to her hips, he caught a glimpse of slender white thigh and the mysterious dark triangle at the confluence of her legs. He swallowed hard and lifted his back off the bed as she struggled to pull down his jeans and briefs. Alicia had never seen a naked man before, and, for a long, heart-stopping minute she simply stared at the vulnerable male power of him.

Then, knowing that nothing had ever felt so right, she tenderly took him in her hands and lowered herself on to him.

She winced as a dart of pain shot through her as he entered her, and then it was gone, quickly forgotten. Leaving her with only the most pleasurable of sensations. She could feel him inside her, filling her, touching something deep within the coils of her femininity, which she just knew was going to drive her wild. Wonderfully wild.

Jared gasped and bucked, the tightness of her a molten, sweet captivity that satisfied everything that he was.

'Alicia,' he said again, beginning to move slowly, carefully, gently thrusting his hips up and then down, introducing her to the dance of love; all the while, his eyes were fixed on her face, alert to any sign of fear, or pain, or withdrawal.

But there was only a growing smile, a sweet expression of concentrated pleasure as she began to ride him with eager confidence, with breath-taking ease, her hands curling around his hips in a possessive grip, her head thrown back, her raven locks tumbling over her shoulders.

She could feel her toes digging into the mattress as the tightening, spiralling intensity drove her upwards, towards the ultimate fulfilment. She threw her head back even further, the line of her throat taut and tense.

Jared's own head began to roll from side to side on his pillow, passion highlighting his cheekbones.

He bit his lip, clenched his jaw, held back, held back, held back until he felt her spasm atop him. She cried out his name then, a pure, sweet, uninhibited sound. 'Jared!' Jared felt tears spring to his eyes as she collapsed on top of him, as he felt his own climax claim him. His arms came out to catch her as she fell. As his arms would now always come out to catch her whenever she fell . . .

SIXTEEN

Davina reached for the dark blue velvet scarf and draped it around her neck. She was wearing a navy-blue dress, in a material which clung like a tenacious lover to every rounded curve of hip and breast.

With her blonde silky hair and cat-green eyes complemented by blue eyeshadow and mascara, she was the centre of attention as she walked into the half-full theatre half an hour later, Gareth Lacey by her side, escorting her to one of the best seats in the front row.

The wife of the provost of a neighbouring college was wearing silk and pearls. St Bede's own don in Oriental Studies was wearing a traditional kimono with diamonds. Men, inevitably, wore black tie. The St Bede's Easter play was always an excuse to push the boat out. Before it had even begun, the Jared Cowan/Alicia Norman play was socially the biggest hit in many years.

Already, Neville Norman, who'd arrived early, was being feted by the contingent from the local press and media.

Gareth, aware that almost every male eye in the room was fixed on Davina as they followed her progress to her seat, found himself smiling slightly. For all the no doubt erotic fantasies going on in lots of those male minds right at that moment, he doubted any one of them had any true concept of the kind of woman Davina actually was. He knew that beneath that bold fashionable front lay shyness. Underneath that strident intellect was — to use an old-fashioned phrase — a thoroughly decent human being, capable of great depths of compassion and human understanding. Behind that sophisticated, well-travelled, world-weary facade lay the woman who'd worked for a charity in Africa for over a year in appalling conditions. A woman who still donated ten percent of her earnings (big or small) to charity, because of her hatred of social injustice and poverty.

And, above all, Gareth knew that she was a woman capable of more emotion than many of those men watching her so avidly could possibly appreciate. Or deal with.

Davina sat down and shot him a careful look out of the corner of her eye. He was saying nothing about her refusal to move in with him. Hadn't even attempted to persuade her to change her mind. And it worried her. Was he tired of her already? The thought made her burn with impotent fury and froze her in pain. Never had a man got under her skin like this.

Gareth leaned back in his chair, a devastatingly handsome picture of maleness. The blackness of his dinner jacket, teamed with a dazzling white shirt, highlighted the dark silvery grey of his eyes, and the shining darkness of his hair. He slipped on his reading glasses to study the souvenir programme while Davina had to physically fight the urge to move across the seat, sit on his lap, loop her arms around his neck and demand to know that he still loved her.

Instead she forced herself to think about Gavin Brock. If all had gone well, he'd already handed in his essay, with the page from the stolen exam paper concealed inside it. Even now, for all she knew, his teacher might be marking his work, finding it . . .

* * *

Backstage, the cast were already dressed, and Alicia watched them in growing alarm. 'Relax!' Emily gave her friend a wide smile. 'It'll be just fine.'

'Ten minutes to curtain!' the call went out, and somebody giggled nervously. Alicia could stand it no longer.

'I'm going to find Jared,' she murmured, and set off. Jared, dressed in a smart pair of black trousers and a well-ironed blue shirt that looked oddly endearing on him, was talking to the prompter. Jared saw her, and his face lit up. He hurried across to her, taking her hands in his the moment they met. They felt cold. 'You all right?' he asked softly.

'Uh-uh,' she shook her head. 'I'm terrified.'

'You look stunning,' he told her sincerely, hoping to distract her. And she did. She was dressed in a dark trouser suit with wide lapels and a very feminine, cream silk camisole underneath. Her long black hair was swept up in a mass of curls at the back of her head, with two single tendrils falling past her ears, framing her lovely face. Her blue eyes were rounded with fear and excitement.

'Have you seen . . .' Jared began, lowering his voice instinctively, 'Rupert?'

'Not since this morning,' Alicia admitted quickly. 'Jared, I think he noticed I wasn't wearing the ring.'

Jared nodded. He looked worried, but he smiled reassuringly. 'Well, we always knew he might. Have you sent it back to Warrington yet?'

'No. I haven't had a chance to find a decent courier yet — it's worth an absolute fortune, I can't just trust it to anyone. But . . .'

'There you are!' The cultured voice had them both jumping apart. Jared's face firmed as he looked up to see Rupert approaching. He was dressed in the character of Sam Blake, the lover and murderer of the play's victim.

'Rupert,' Alicia said, glad beyond measure of Jared's presence beside her. 'All set?'

'Of course,' he said pointedly, glancing coldly at Jared. 'Hadn't you better give your pep talk to the others?'

Jared smiled, but shook his head. He had no intention of leaving Alicia alone with the other man. Ever. 'No, they know what they have to do. You've got the best part in the play, you know. We're all relying on you.' As he said it, he wondered nervously if he had done the right thing, diverting Rupert's attention to the play.

Rupert beamed. 'Of course, I won't let you down,' he turned to Alicia, stepping closer, his eyes caressing her.

Alicia had to make herself look at him. Had to swallow back an absurd feeling of guilt. She and Jared had found out that day that Rupert's Moral Tutor was in fact the Reverend Rex Jimson-Clarke, and they had an appointment to see him tomorrow.

'Well, I suppose I'd better take my seat out front,' Alicia said, edging towards the side exit. But as she did so, Rupert glanced down pointedly at her hand.

'Where is my ring, Alicia? Have you lost it?' he asked, then shrugged. 'It's quite valuable. But I won't be angry,' he promised her.

Alicia swallowed hard. 'Er . . . no, I haven't lost it,' she said quietly. 'It was . . . too tight. It hurt my finger.'

'Oh?' Rupert's face brightened. 'Well, in that case, I can have it made bigger.'

Jared stepped in firmly and gave Alicia's hand a comforting squeeze.

'We really have very little time left,' he said, carefully keeping his voice level. 'I must insist you take your place with the others, Rupert.'

Rupert glanced at him, a rather puzzled look in his eyes.

'Place?' he echoed blankly.

'On stage — for the play,' Jared prompted him. Still Rupert looked puzzled. And suddenly, both Jared and Alicia had the same agonised thought at exactly the same moment.

He's forgotten the play!

Then his face seemed to clear. 'Oh! Places. Right.' He smiled brightly. 'Don't worry, darling.' He stepped forward and, before either of them could stop him, kissed Alicia briefly on the forehead. 'I'll be magnificent for you.'

As he moved back, he noticed that they were holding hands. Why were they holding hands? Alicia was his, wasn't she? He moved slowly, clearly confused.

Rupert let himself be led by the director, but his mind whirled. She was his, wasn't she? He could have sworn he'd given her a ring. At the ball. The ball had happened, hadn't it? Sometimes, he knew, he could forget things. Whole days, sometimes. But he was over that now. He couldn't have imagined it all . . .

He felt his head begin to ache.

'Rupert . . . everything will be all right, you know,' Jared said softly, his voice heavy with pity, and he felt a sudden wave of anger towards the boy's father. What kind of man would send his son, in a condition like this, away from home and into an environment as full of pressure as Oxford?

'Oh, I know it'll be all right,' Rupert assured him brightly. He rattled off his first line, to show the director he had nothing to fear. Rupert Greyling-Simms would not let them down.

* * *

Alicia took her seat next to her brother, three down from Davina Granger and Dr Lacey. Neville said nothing as she took her place, but Alicia vowed to have a very firm word with him later. They had bank accounts and non-existent bribes to talk about. The lights began to dim.

Alicia felt her heart race. The heavy green curtains moved smoothly apart, and instantly the audience was in the small kitchen of a house on a run-down estate. Emily, in the character of Susan Smart, was cooking dinner for her husband and her glowering, unhappy son.

The annual St Bede's Easter play was under way.

When the final curtain came down there was instant and immediate applause. Davina Granger was the first to get to her feet, and several people instantly followed suit. The play had been well written, acted, managed and directed. The social comment had been just astringent enough to make some members of the audience feel uncomfortable, the puzzle of the murder mystery itself just clever enough to be satisfying without being too gimmicky. The emotional scenes had been fraught, and cleverly acted.

Alicia, who'd watched her work unfold with a growing sense of relief and disbelief, felt herself too weak to stand, now that it was finally over.

As the cast began to take their individual bows, Rupert received the loudest cheers and applause of them all. And Alicia knew he deserved it. His portrayal of Sam Blake, the jilted lover, driven by desperation, through rejection and jealousy, to an explosive act of violence, had been worthy of any professional actor. There were cries of 'Director', and suddenly there was Jared, bounding on to the stage, taking a brief bow, and then calls for 'Author'. Dazed, Alicia found herself pushed on to the stage. The lights were bright and hot, and she glanced out nervously at the sea of clapping and cheering people before giving a brief and awkward bow.

Rupert watched it all. He felt calm now. He knew what he had to do. He'd begun to understand it, in the second act. When he was trying to persuade his lover to leave her husband, and she wouldn't. Now, watching Alicia and Jared taking their bows, he could see it all absolutely clearly.

He knew why they'd been holding hands. They were lovers. But he couldn't allow her to marry *him*, Rupert, and then keep Jared as a lover. He knew now what he must do. It was all so clear. So obvious. Alicia had written a part for him. A man in love with a woman who didn't love him enough to sacrifice her selfish needs and desires to be with him. A woman who must die because of that. Oh yes. Rupert knew what he had to do now.

He smiled, a sudden dazzling flash of perfect teeth, and along with the rest of the cast, took his final bow.

* * *

'Well, what do you think?' Alicia asked her brother as they stood in the middle of the SCR, accepting canapés from the passing butler. 'Did you like the play or not?'

'It was a good play,' he said shortly. 'And Rupert's performance was uncannily accurate.'

Alicia's chin lifted. 'I'm mad at you,' she said just as shortly. 'That stunt you pulled, putting money into Jared's bank account without his knowledge . . . you should be ashamed of yourself.'

Neville was, and muttered an apology.

'So you'll support me when I tell Dad that I'm not going to work for the magazine? That I'm going to write crime novels instead?' she challenged.

Neville looked appalled. He muttered and wriggled some more, but eventually agreed that, perhaps, she should be free to choose her own path. Then he excused himself with the plea that he needed to type up his review notes.

The rest of the party hardly noticed Neville's absence. Davina Granger was holding court in one corner while Gareth watched, smiling, apparently not at all offended that she was getting more attention than he was. Everyone was happy.

Even Rupert was content. He'd just spotted a small, sharp knife on the fruit platter. It bore the St Bede's crest of arms on the handle and had obviously been made by a craftsman. He lifted the knife casually and studied it.

It was old. It was made of the finest silver. He smiled and nodded. Fate, again, was with him. Showing him the way. Casually, he slipped it into his jacket pocket.

It was indeed the perfect knife with which to kill his beloved.

SEVENTEEN

Jack Carter yawned over his sixth cup of coffee. He'd been up since six marking a pile of essays and needed a break. But his job as English teacher at King Canute College was his first appointment, and he was totally dedicated to his work.

He pulled the next essay to him, reading the name on the top sheet with a little sigh of disappointment. Gavin Brock was not one of King Canute's brighter students.

He ploughed through an uninspired essay on Hardy's *Tess of the D'Urbervilles*, sighing over a passage which he recognised as being plagiarised from a critical piece by Bolton, taken almost word for word. But then he turned the next page and found himself going cold with shock.

Instead of looking down on yet more of Mr Brock's rather untidy scrawl, he found himself face to face with a very neat, photocopied page of exam questions.

Slowly, he lowered his coffee cup. It was from this year's syllabus. And the little line of figures at the bottom of the page bore the code numbers of this year's finals. Jack felt the colour drain from his face. He stood up, then abruptly sat down again. He knew what this meant. He knew the dreadful ramifications . . .

He read the questions through again, frantic, sure he'd made a mistake. Hoping that he'd made a mistake. But he hadn't.

Finally, Jack gathered all the essays together and put them in his briefcase. After a brief hesitation, he slipped the photocopied exam paper inside too and snapped the locks shut.

Then he saw the time, gave a muffled yelp, and dashed for his bus. He'd be late for college if he wasn't careful.

* * *

Davina awoke and lay gazing up at the familiar, age-dappled ceiling. She sighed, feeling deeply depressed. Soon she would leave this pleasant set of rooms for good. Even the anthology was complete, as she'd chosen the final poems last week. Nothing was holding her back.

It was only Gareth who kept her here now. She got up and pulled on faded jeans and her baby-pink cashmere sweater. She combed her hair, and slowly, reluctantly met the reflection of her green eyes in the glass. The woman looking back at her was almost a stranger.

I look desperate, Davina thought, with a jolt of nasty surprise. I look . . . haunted. She turned away, pacing the room. She had things to do. Except . . . she didn't. All she had to occupy her time now was waiting for disaster to strike. And watch it overtake him. Gareth.

She strode angrily to the kitchen and made herself a bitter cup of strong black coffee. Forgot the sugar. Cursed, and put some in. Drank it down as if it were poison, then paced some more. She glanced at her watch. It was eight fifteen.

David. Think about David. Davina passed the mirror again. Stopped. Looked at herself. No good. She still looked like a woman going to the gallows. She rubbed her hand wearily across her eyes. They felt hot and gritty.

Just because she loved him didn't mean she had to spare him. For centuries women had been classed as the weaker sex.

The sex that couldn't see a job through when the going got tough. The sex who didn't have enough brains in their heads to vote. The sex who got paid less for doing the same jobs as a man, just because a woman was intrinsically worth less.

Except . . . 'Damn!' she yelled. She snatched up her bag and raced to the door and out into Wolsey's hall, heading straight to the public phone booth. She had Gavin Brock's number in her purse and she ferreted it out grimly.

'Yeah?' the voice was wary.

'Gavin? It's me. I want you to hold off putting the exam paper into the essay.' There. She'd said it. Done it. Betrayed her brother. Betrayed her own sense of self-worth. Sold her concept of justice down the river. All because she was a woman in love, acting like all other women in love had done, down through the ages. She should be feeling terrible. Not wilting as a massive load seemed to slip off her shoulders.

'I can't, I gave it to Mr Carter yesterday.'

Davina took a deep breath. She closed her eyes for a moment, then nodded. She leaned her head slowly against the wall and swallowed hard. The plaster felt grave-cold against her forehead. 'Oh. In that case . . . forget it,' she said flatly. She hung up quickly, cutting off his protests. She slowly turned, letting her back thump against the wall. She felt physically as well as mentally exhausted.

She managed a grim, weak laugh. So, it was done after all. Fate had taken the decision out of her hands. Just as well, perhaps. She walked slowly back to her room.

Met her eyes in the mirror again. Began to pace again . . .

* * *

Jack Carter jogged along the corridor. 'Oh, Mr Thorpe!' He sprinted to catch up with the head of English. 'Sorry,' he gasped. 'Just wanted to catch you . . . before . . . you went . . . in. I wondered if you knew who was setting this year's papers in the Modern Poetry finals?' Jack decided the best approach was to simply ask outright.

Mr Thorpe glanced impatiently at his watch. 'Moderns? Oh, that'll be Dr Gareth Lacey. One of your Oxford lot, I understand. Now, I must get on . . .'

Jack was barely aware of the older man, leaving him with a muttered apology to push his way into the packed lecture hall.

Slowly, numbly, Jack turned back, moving much more slowly down the corridor than he'd come up it. He himself was free until eleven. He made his way to the common room, not surprised to see it deserted in mid-morning. He slumped down in a chair, the briefcase in his hand.

Jack Carter had indeed gone to Oxford, but not to St Bede's. Nevertheless, he knew Gareth Lacey well. Had attended every lecture the man ever gave, with Jack often staying behind afterwards to chat to the great man. He'd liked him.

Jack scowled, knowing he should go straight to Mr Morgan, King Canute's principal, with what he had in his briefcase.

But he didn't. Instead he walked to the telephone and called St Bede's.

* * *

Davina went to the bank and drew out a large amount of cash. The teller was nervous on her behalf, but she simply stuffed the money into her bag and left. Back in her room she waited until the lunch hour, then called King Canute, getting herself put through to the refectory. There a very helpful dinner lady agreed to page Gavin Brock. A minute or two later, and he was on the phone.

'Yeah?'

'It's me again. I want you to get the exam paper back.'

Gavin swore. Davina waited patiently until he'd finished. Now that she'd made up her mind as to what she must do, she felt calm once more. 'I've got another five thousand pounds in cash in my purse. Just waiting for you to come and collect it,' she said simply. 'All you have to do is bring me the exam paper back.'

There was a considerable silence on the other end. Then, 'What if I can't get it back? Suppose he's already found the paper . . .'

Davina bit her lip. 'All right. If he's found the paper, I want you to call me straight away.' She rattled off the number of Wolsey Hall. 'If that's the case, I don't want you to even mention Dr Lacey. Tell him you don't know how the paper came to be there. You didn't even notice it.'

'Oh yeah. Right! Like he's going to believe that!'

Davina sighed. 'Gavin, you get your extra money, whether he believes it or not. All you've got to do is keep your mouth shut. OK?'

'OK,' Gavin said cheerfully and rang off.

In the cool hall of Wolsey Davina slowly hung up. Then she went back to her room. And cried. Bitterly.

* * *

Gareth parked his car in the King Canute's car park, and within moments was being met by Jack Carter and escorted inside. 'Jack! Good to see you again. How are things going?' he asked pleasantly.

He was still a little puzzled as to what he was doing here. Jack had rung him up only an hour ago, saying he needed to see him urgently. Gareth, who remembered him from past lectures, had been surprised. Now he frowned slightly. 'Jack, you look terrible. Has something happened?'

Jack sighed and steered Gareth into a small alcove under the main stairs, where a group of chairs was set around a low coffee table. There he reached into his briefcase. 'Dr Lacey, I found this paper this morning, in one of my students' essays.'

Gareth glanced down at the document in question, and the colour drained dramatically from his face as he recognised it.

166

'What the hell . . . ?' Gareth said inelegantly. He quickly ran his eyes down the list of multiple-choice questions. 'I don't understand this,' he said, clearly bewildered. 'I sent the papers to your principal last week. By courier. They should have been locked in his safe straight away.'

Jack nodded. 'That's what I thought. Mr Morgan's very punctilious about exam papers. I just don't know what to do!'

Gareth stood up decisively. 'We have to go and see him right away. If the papers have been compromised . . .'

'Oh, Mr Carter! There you are.' Gavin Brock, bounding down the stairs, beamed in pleasure at having tracked down his prey. He gave the man beside his teacher a brief, uninterested look. 'I wanted to ask you if I could have my essay back,' he began guilelessly.

'This is the student I was telling you about,' Jack whispered abruptly to Gareth as Gavin approached.

Gareth felt himself stiffen, then thrust out his hand, leaving Gavin no other choice but to shake it.

'Oh, yes. Er . . . Gavin Brock, this is Dr Gareth Lacey,' Jack introduced them. And the effect of Gareth's name on Gavin was immediate. He actually took a step back. Went deathly pale. Looking into Gareth's astute, level grey eyes, Gavin became suddenly very afraid. Very afraid indeed.

'I want to have a word with you, Mr Brock,' Gareth said softly. 'About an exam paper.'

Gavin gulped and immediately folded. 'It's all her fault!' he wailed. 'I had nothing to do with it! She offered me money. She brought the photocopy. I . . .'

Gareth's eyes narrowed. Grimly he lowered the shaking boy into another of the chairs. 'Now,' he said, his voice ominously quiet. 'I suggest you start at the beginning. Start with exactly who "she" is.'

* * *

Davina was already packing when Gareth got back to St Bede's. He didn't bother knocking on her door but opened it silently. He closed it just as silently again behind him, then leaned against it, watching her pack.

There was no expression whatsoever on his face.

Only the stormy shadows in his grey eyes reflected the bitter pain of hurt bewilderment he was feeling.

Davina tossed the last of her things — the long white dress — into her holdall and zipped it shut with a final jerking movement. She hoisted it off the bed and looked slowly around. She was going to miss St Bede's. The place had a charm that had wormed its way into her very soul.

She shrugged, turned, and froze.

Gareth glanced from her suddenly tense, wary face to her bag, then back again. 'Leaving?' he asked softly.

This time it was the turn of Davina's hackles to rise, very slowly. Menace was in the room with her. The presence of a man on the hunt. She swallowed nervously, then elevated her chin. The defiant gesture was so typical of her. So Davina. Gareth felt his heart contract. Even now, even knowing that all this time she'd been plotting to destroy him, he loved her. Part of him, a purely primitive part, even felt elated. She'd hated him enough to stalk him. Spent so much emotion on him. A savage, primordial part of him could feel a sexual kick of awareness. He felt, absurdly, honoured. But that was not all he felt. He felt rage, too. And pain. So much pain. He'd thought she loved him, in her own unique, complicated way. To find that she never had was almost more than he could bear.

'Yes, I'm leaving,' Davina confirmed. 'As you can see,' she added loftily, swinging the holdall by her side.

'You've finished the anthology?'

'Of course.'

Gareth's lips twisted. 'Of course. Far be it from the great Davina Granger to leave a job undone.'

Davina's green eyes flickered. What . . . ?

'Weren't you even going to say goodbye?' Gareth asked calmly. 'Don't I even merit a "So long, sucker, thanks for the memory"?'

168

Davina shrugged. It was curious. She could actually feel her heart breaking inside her. And yet she was out of herself. Feeling hardly anything at all. 'All right,' she said softly. 'So long, sucker. Thanks for the memory.'

Gareth laughed. 'Oh, Davina. You're a classic, you know that?'

She laughed too. But she was still feeling nothing. Nothing at all. The numbness was wonderful. But somehow, she didn't think it was going to last for ever. She had to get out of there now. Before the pain came. Before she could no longer hide the fact that she loved him. Before she blurted out the whole sordid truth.

'Oh, for pity's sake, Gareth,' she said mockingly. 'Don't tell me you don't know when an affair's over? It was very nice and all that, and I'll always remember you with affection. OK?' She put one hand on her hip. 'Can I go now?'

Gareth smiled at her. 'In just a minute. First I want to know why you wanted me broken.'

Davina blinked. 'What?' she asked faintly.

Gareth walked slowly towards her. 'You heard me,' he said softly. 'I want to know what I ever did to you, Davina, to make you come after me.'

Davina dropped the holdall. Suddenly, all the numbness was gone.

The battlefield was now even.

EIGHTEEN

They'd all agreed to meet up in the theatre again at three o'clock the next afternoon in order to read the reviews, and Alicia, dressed in a demure tartan skirt and plain white blouse, clutched the sheaf of newspapers to her breast as she hurried along through Wallace Quad towards Webster.

Rupert Greyling-Simms watched her from his vantage point high up in Hall, and then slowly lowered his binoculars. He felt much better this morning. With the decision about what to do with his life taken out of his hands, he felt much calmer. All the despair caused by his uncertainty was just a distant memory. It was all due to Alicia. He would thank her properly. Soon. Very soon.

In the theatre, the cast swooped on Alicia and her newspapers the moment she set foot in the door. There was a general sound of frantic page-turning, and then the usual 'listen to this bit', and 'look what he said about me' groans and 'I can't believe I'm in the papers' jubilance.

Alicia read Neville's review aloud.

"'The annual St Bede's Easter play was shown last night and differed vastly from previous productions. Firstly, the play was not culled from the extensive college library, but was written especially for the purpose by Alicia Norman, a first-year English Literature student. Secondly, St Bede's daringly opted to try a much more modern approach than in previous years, putting on a very nice little murder mystery.'"

The review went on to praise the staging. Then continued:

"'The play itself was moderately well written, with a strong cast of characters, a brave modern setting, and a fairly intriguing plot. It's a pity the second act, instead of bolstering the first and making way for the third, became a little bogged down. If the director had shorn off a good ten minutes in the middle of the play, the balance would have been a lot better.'"

'I knew he'd have to get a dig in somewhere,' Jared murmured gloomily. Alicia glanced up at him, caught his eye and grinned widely. Jared, unabashed, grinned back.

Neville rounded it off with a few more pithy and pertinent comments, and Alicia sighed with relief. It could have been so much worse! Jared was shaking his head. 'Well, well, well. Who'd have believed it? A word of praise for nearly everyone.'

Rupert, who'd just that moment come through the door, watched the teasing by-play with a stab of pain that was almost exquisite. He walked slowly forward, watching the couple out of the corner of his eye as the rest of the cast greeted him.

'You're a hit, Rupe,' someone called over to him, and Alicia and Jared both quickly looked up. A feeling of anxiety settled on them as they watched Rupert smiling and joining in with the rest of the cast's revelry.

Alicia bent her head towards Jared. 'What are we going to do?' she murmured, keeping a wary eye on Rupert, who showed no signs, at the moment, of coming over to them. She wished, guiltily, that she didn't feel so scared of him, so unhappy whenever he was around.

'We'll go and find Mr Jimson-Clarke,' Jared said firmly. 'You know he's arranged for us to see him in chapel. He's rehearsing the Easter service.'

Alicia nodded. 'Let's go now then?' she urged him, her face pale, her eyes huge. 'We shouldn't wait any longer.'

'No,' Jared agreed sombrely. 'I don't think we should.'

Alicia nodded and they left quietly. So quietly that when Rupert looked up to check on them, he found only a pair of empty seats instead. His heart lurched. Instantly, his hand went to the inside pocket of his raincoat, where he fingered the knife lovingly. Its cold sharp blade reassured him. No matter where they'd gone, he'd catch up with them again . . .

* * *

Rex Jimson-Clarke glanced up as the chapel door opened and smiled. But his long years of experience told him instantly that something was amiss.

As they finally reached the front pew, their footsteps echoing eerily in the cold room, Jared glanced at Alicia anxiously, reassured by her calm, if pale face.

Rex beamed at them. 'Good afternoon,' he said cheerfully. He patted the space on the intricately carved wooden pew beside him. 'Now. What can I do for you?'

Both the younger people noticed a certain steadiness in the man's teddy-bear face. An integrity in the brown eyes that was comforting rather than off-putting. Jared and Alicia sat down. Jared looked at her, raising an eyebrow. Will you, or will I?

Alicia took a deep breath and began to speak.

* * *

When they left the chapel nearly an hour later, they both felt infinitely better. Sadder, but better.

Rex Jimson-Clarke had heard Alicia out without interruption, without shock, surprise or censure as she told him about Rupert. They'd both been worried that Rupert's title and money might influence the man, but Rex Jimson-Clarke only asked one or two pertinent questions and then sat in quiet, thoughtful silence. Finally he'd thanked them for bringing the problem to his attention and assured them he would handle matters from there. He advised them to keep out of Rupert's way, and, at all costs, to avoid any kind of confrontation with him. Relieved, they'd promised to do as he asked, and now, walking across the lawns towards Jared's room, they found themselves almost light-headed with relief. At last, it was no longer their burden alone. They both trusted Rex to do something to help Rupert. There had been a generous strength to the man that had impressed them both.

* * *

A glint of light coming from one of the tall multi-paned windows in Hall reflected off Rupert's binoculars as he followed their progress through the gardens. He knew he'd pick them up again. It had been written in the stars long ago . . .

* * *

Jared's room faced the main college gardens, and as soon as they were inside, he went to the small cupboard beside his bed. His room was neat, his bed in apple-pie order.

'You'll make someone a good husband one day,' Alicia said cheekily, running a mocking finger across the top of his rather battered desk, and smiling when it came away clean.

'Is that a proposal?' Jared shot back, straightening up with a bottle of champagne in one hand and a carton of orange juice in the other. 'I thought we'd toast our success with Buck's Fizz. Remember the first time?' he added softly.

Instantly, the afternoon in the punt sprang back to her mind. The weeping willows screening them. The duck that had quacked for some bread. Their first, long, lingering kiss . . . She took a deep breath. 'I'll never forget it,' she assured him softly.

Jared smiled and poured the champagne and orange juice into two mugs. 'Sorry, but the crystal glasses have gone back to the chap who loaned them to me.'

She accepted the mug as if it were a fragile glass nonetheless and solemnly clinked it against Jared's. 'To the success of the play,' Jared murmured.

'To us,' Alicia corrected softly. 'And yes. Actually, that was a proposal.'

Jared blinked, his clear brown eyes going blank for a few seconds, and then he flushed. His eyes glowed. 'You mean . . . ?'

Alicia nodded. 'Yes. Jared Cowan, will you marry me?'

'Yes.'

For a second neither of them moved. Neither spoke. Then, slowly, Jared placed his drink on the table and reached for hers. It left her fingers unresistingly and she watched, her heart thumping, as he placed her mug beside his own.

'Come here,' he said softly. Alicia took a slow step forward. Then another one. Then she was in his arms. He reached for her, drawing her gently to him, loving the way the curve of her hip fitted against his own. The way his arm rested exactly at the curve of her waist. The way her nipples, clearly visible beneath the demure cream top, reacted to the touch of his own hot flesh. He looked into those lovely blue eyes, full of love, of confidence, of happiness, and felt his own eyes fill with tears.

'I'm so happy, I can't . . . say . . .' he began, his voice trembling.

Alicia nodded. She was a writer, but she didn't have the right words for this moment either. 'Kiss me,' she said softly. And he willingly complied.

* * *

Rupert's hands clenched around the binoculars as he watched them from Hall. His knuckles gleamed palely in the waning afternoon sunshine. Oh, Alicia. Don't! Please — don't . . .

* * *

Rex Jimson-Clarke knocked on the principal's door and went in. Sin-Jun looked up and smiled encouragingly. 'Rex! How's everything going with the Easter service?'

Rex slumped wearily down in the chair opposite the principal's desk, and Sin-Jun felt his smile fall away.

'Trouble?' he asked brusquely.

Rex nodded. 'I'm afraid so.'

* * *

Alicia looped her arms around Jared's neck, melting into his kiss as though she were wading into a warm swimming pool. She ran her fingers through his crisp dark hair, loving the way the mass of waves felt in her hand, tickling her fingertips and warming her palms.

He smelled of pine forest and male arousal. She could feel the power in his arms as they held her tight and gloried in the differences of their respective strengths. He might be able to crush her physically, but she knew all that male power was actually there to protect her. To guide her. To lean on in times of trouble. Jared's hand splayed across her spine, his fingers covering almost the whole of her back. She felt fragile in his arms, and yet she filled them, as no other woman ever had, or ever would. Slowly, reluctantly, with sighs of regret, their lips parted. 'I want to kiss you like that for ever,' Alicia murmured.

Jared nodded. 'I know what you mean,' he said gruffly. And lowered his lips again. It was not possible, of course, to kiss for ever . . . but, in that instant, he was willing to try . . .

* * *

Rupert leaned against the pane of glass, feeling its coldness chill his skin, making him shiver uncontrollably. The binoculars began to shake, making the image of the lovers, locked in their private kiss, tremble in a kaleidoscope of colours. Tears ran down his face.

'No more, Alicia,' he whispered. 'Please. No more.'

* * *

Jared lifted his lips from Alicia's, his eyes reluctantly opening. Her head was pressed against his shoulder, her rapid shallow breaths making her breasts rise and fall against his chest, causing him to shudder in reaction to every intimate touch of her nipples. She looked up at him then, caught the expression in his eyes, and felt her own body tighten. She led him to the bed, and as they dropped on to it, they fell out of sight of the man watching them.

'Jared,' she whispered, as he lay gently on top of her, his elbows resting on either side of her neck as he looked down at her.

'What?'

'Nothing.' She shook her head, her mass of black hair spreading like a fan across his pillow. 'Just . . . Jared.'

He dipped his head and caught one nipple in his mouth through her blouse. She gasped, arching her back off the bed as twin rivers of fire spread from her breasts and lodged in that secret, waiting, aching place at the very core of her womanhood. She felt him release the zip of her skirt, moving the material aside, his fingers tracing a circular pattern from her knee to her thigh, his caress warm and knowing. She sighed, and let her legs fall apart. Gently he stroked his thumb over her yearning flesh, and she cried out softly, biting her lip, closing her eyes, lost in the sensation of his touch. She writhed, her whole body following the movement of his thumb, and when she cried out and shuddered, her beautiful face rose-pink from the growing heat building inside her, Jared thought she had never looked more beautiful.

Her eyes opened, as blue and sparkling as perfect sapphires. She reached up and cupped his face with her hands. 'Your turn,' she said softly, and moved her hand down between them. He gasped as she unzipped his jeans and took him in her hand. He threw his head back, swallowing convulsively. He collapsed against her. His cheek pillowed to her breast, his body as taut as a violin string as she felt him harden helplessly.

After several long minutes of exquisite torture, he groaned, spasmed, then lay still, his breath harsh as he gulped for air. Slowly their bodies cooled. Eventually he raised himself on one elbow again, propping the side of his face against his hand as he looked down at her.

'Well, how do you think you're going to enjoy life as Mrs Cowan?'

Alicia opened sleepy, contented, half-satiated eyes. She reached for his shirt buttons and began to undress him in earnest. 'I'll tell you later,' she murmured throatily.

* * *

Rupert Greyling-Simms swayed against the window. His binoculars fell forgotten from his hand and hit the wooden floorboards with a clatter. He raised stricken eyes to the window where he knew they were together, and bit back a wailing cry that seemed to rise up from the very depths of him. And then, as abruptly as it came, the desire to scream at the world left him. Instead, he began to smile.

Of course. He should have known Alicia was only doing what she had to do. He should have trusted her. She and Jared had to do . . . this thing . . . to him.

He was the betrayed lover. In order to fulfil their destinies, in order to make their play real, she had to . . . spend this afternoon like this. With him.

She must know he was watching. Must have chosen this moment especially. Of course. It was time! How stupid he was being. How lucky he was to have Alicia to guide him.

Rupert waited, as patient as the wind, until he saw her re-emerge into the gardens and make her way across them, back to her own room in Webster. Then he checked the knife in his pocket. It felt reassuringly solid to his touch. In a world dissolving around him, that knife felt wonderfully real.

Alicia. Oh, Alicia . . . it's time at last.

As he stepped into Webster and began to mount the stairs to her room, he was smiling. Rupert felt good.

* * *

In his office, Sin-Jun rang two telephone numbers. The first connected him to the Earl of Warrington, of whom he asked some very pertinent questions which demanded some very difficult answers. And, having got those from the very reluctant Earl, the second call was to a psychiatrist Sin-Jun knew who was attached to the John Radcliffe Hospital, and who had the power to order a committal, should it be necessary.

Both calls were, of course, made when it was already far too late . . .

NINETEEN

At about the same time as Jared and Alicia parted, Davina Granger watched with fatalistic eyes as Gareth began to walk towards her. She backed a few steps away. Her heart was thumping with a mixture of fear, dread and delight. Although she'd planned to slip out of Oxford like a ghost, she couldn't help but feel elated that she was to see him one last time. Even though it was agony.

Gareth smiled at her grimly. 'Davina!' he chided cruelly. 'You're not afraid of me, surely?' he asked softly. 'You? Who are afraid of nothing and nobody?'

Davina shrugged one shoulder. 'You've always been someone to fear, Gareth,' she admitted quietly. But not because she thought he might physically harm her. She knew him better than that. Gareth Lacey would never hit a woman. No. The danger was not physical. It was mental. Spiritual.

Gareth's grey eyes darkened, as if a cloud had moved across some internal sun. 'And what, exactly, do you mean by that?'

When he'd listened to Gavin Brock pour forth his stream of accusations, he simply hadn't wanted to believe him, but finally he had been forced to the conclusion that this nightmare was real. Only then had he begun to think. To reason. Coldly. Logically. Rationally.

Who else could come and go in his room without suspicion as easily as Davina? Who else would dare to do something so outrageous? Only Davina. His unique, bold, yet humanly flawed . . . Davina.

As he watched her back away from him, a strange mixture of defiance and pain on her face, he had the grim feeling that he'd been very stupid. Somewhere, somehow, he'd been very stupid indeed.

'You came here expressly to set up the exam paper scam, didn't you?' he asked quietly. He had to physically fight the urge to go to her and shake her, and demand to know why, why, why? At the same time, he wanted to carry her to that bed and make love to her with savagery and passion until they were both exhausted.

To think that it had all been a sham. All their wonderful conversations. All their shared intimacies. Even the poem she'd written for him — 'The Flame Moth' — was a sham. Lies. None of it had been real. That's what was killing him . . . He shook his head. He had to get things straight in his mind. He had to put his world back on to some sort of orbit if he was to make any sense of Davina at all.

'Yes,' she admitted quietly. 'I came here to destroy you.' She swallowed back a huge aching lump in her throat as she spoke. He looked so . . . hurt. So bewildered. She knew she should be glad. Fiercely glad. It must have been the way David had felt for so long. This was the revenge she'd come seeking. So why was it like ashes in her mouth?

She knew why. It was because she loved him. Had loved him for a long time. She took a deep breath. 'Why don't you just let me go, Gareth?' she said quietly. 'It would be easiest. For both of us.'

Gareth nodded. 'Oh yes. Undoubtedly it would be easiest.' He cocked his head very slightly to one side, and a small, sad smile turned his lips upwards. 'But when have we ever done anything the easy way, Davina?' he murmured.

Davina sighed.

'So, you came here to destroy me — and part of that was to make me love you. Wasn't it, Davina?'

'Yes.'

Gareth nodded. 'You succeeded very well.'

Davina laughed grimly. 'That's nothing to brag about,' she snarled back. 'I fell for you too.'

Gareth stopped dead in the room. What? Then he laughed. 'Poor Davina,' he murmured. 'You must have hated every moment of loving me.' He pushed back the dark strands of hair which had fallen into his eyes, and she noticed that his hand was shaking as he did so. 'Are you going to tell me why you've done this to us?' he asked quietly.

In response, Davina walked to her holdall and took out her purse, keeping a wary eye on him as she did so. She offered him a small, rather tattered snapshot. 'It's because of him,' she said softly. 'Everything's because of him.'

Gareth moved just close enough to her to take the small square photograph. He looked down at it, and his face froze. 'David Garrett,' he whispered.

'Yes. David,' Davina said. 'My stepbrother.'

Gareth's head shot up. His eyes fixed on hers, the grey irises contracting. 'Your brother?' Whatever he'd been expecting, it was not this. 'I see . . . that's why I didn't made the connection until now. You didn't share a name.'

'Mum always used to say, "Change the name and not the letter, marry for worse, but not for better",' Davina muttered flippantly. 'Although my stepfather was a sweetie, so she wasn't worse off by marrying him. I think she meant that my father and stepfather not only shared the same initial letter in their surnames, but that mine and David's names were so similar.' She paused, fighting back the tears which always threatened when she thought of her brother. 'I was eight when Mum married Pete Garrett. David was two. His mother died when David was a babe in arms, so he was the baby brother I'd always wanted but never had.'

Gareth looked back at the photograph, a wary expression on his face, then slowly handed it back. 'Just what do you think happened to David, Davina?' he asked quietly.

And Davina found herself stiffening. For there was something else in that lovely voice of his now. And Davina suddenly knew, instinctively, that Gareth Lacey knew something about her brother that she didn't.

And it had her scared. Or rather, it had her cold, logical self running scared. Her heart and spirit, on the other hand, were beginning to stir. To throb and expand with a desperate surge of hope . . .

'Only what his letters told me,' she answered him, but there was something . . . different now. The balance of power had somehow shifted — in Gareth's favour. She shivered.

'And what did those letters tell you?' Gareth asked bleakly.

Davina's lips twisted. 'Read them for yourself. I kept every one.' And she stalked to her holdall, grabbed the pile of letters and thrust them under his nose. But as Gareth read the accusing, bitter pages that told the tale of a young man persecuted by an older, Machiavellian monster, his expression became sadder, not angrier. Or guiltier.

'I see,' he said at last.

Davina swallowed, her mouth suddenly as dry as dust.

'You see?' she echoed, trying to put as much scorn and hate into her voice as she could. 'Is that all you can say?'

Gareth turned to look at her then. All that fire. All for nothing . . . Oh, Davina, he thought despairingly. If only you'd given that fire to me . . .

'I'm saying,' he said quietly, 'that I see now why you came to Oxford to destroy me. Why you chose the exam scam. You wanted to see me exiled from Oxford, yes? To see my reputation destroyed, just as David's was?'

'Yes,' she said. 'You see very well.'

Gareth nodded. 'I have the whole picture now. But you don't.' He said it so matter-of-factly, with absolutely no trace of doubt, that she felt herself rocked. A wave of hideous doubt swept over her. She took a deep breath.

'Are you denying it?' she said at last. 'I thought you might at least spare me your excuses.'

Gareth didn't react to the barb. Instead he stared into her eyes, as if trying to decide something. Eventually he sighed and turned away.

'Do you really want the truth, Davina?' he asked at last. He turned back to her, and her heart lurched. She wanted to believe that he still loved her. As impossible as that hope was, as pointless as it would be even if true, some soul-deep part of her wanted him still to love her.

'Well, Davina?' Gareth asked relentlessly. 'Do you want to know the truth or don't you?'

Davina felt her chin lift in familiar challenge. 'Yes.'

Gareth nodded. He had expected nothing else. 'Then follow me. And I'll show you the truth about your brother, David.'

He led her, without speaking, to his rooms, and there she watched him walk towards the filing cabinet and withdraw a folder. He stood staring down at what was obviously a letter for so long that Davina thought she would scream. Eventually he walked to one of the big leather chairs beside his desk and sat down in it wearily, Davina joining him in the one opposite. He knew he'd already won the battle — but it was a battle he'd never wanted to fight in the first place. All he'd wanted to do was love her.

Well, he could still do that. His grey eyes sparked. Yes. He could still do that! When you brushed away all the misunderstanding, that's what was left. He could still love her! But first, those misunderstandings had to be dealt with. And therein lay the danger. Everything depended on how Davina reacted to the truth. His whole future hung in the balance. Their future. Slowly, Gareth began to speak.

'You never attended the inquest into your brother's death did you, Davina?'

'No,' she said. She hadn't been able to.

'So you don't know the findings of the inquest?'

'No,' she admitted, looking at him levelly. 'Are you telling me they didn't bring it in as suicide?'

'Oh no, they brought it in as suicide,' Gareth concurred. 'But suicide while the balance of his mind was disturbed by the brain tumour the ME had discovered during the autopsy.'

Davina felt the room around her dip, recede, darken. A few moments later she was aware that she was staring down at her feet. A warm hand was pressed against the back of her neck, holding her bent over. She took several long, deep breaths. Then, slowly, gingerly, she leaned back in the chair. Gareth, who'd been kneeling down in front of her, got up and walked to the small kitchen cubby hole, returning with a glass of cold water. He handed it to her and watched her sip it, thankful to see her white cheeks gain a little colour. His heart was racing uncomfortably. He moved back to his chair, waiting for her to give him the sign that she was ready to go on.

At last, Davina put down the glass and turned to look at him. 'Let's finish it,' she whispered bitterly.

Gareth sighed. 'For the last two terms your brother was here, he became prone to mood swings. He lost his friends, because he started to accuse them of things. Trying to steal his girlfriend. Searching his room when he was out. That kind of thing. His work went downhill — his essays became unfocused. Shoddy. His Moral Tutor tried to get him to see a therapist, but he flatly refused. I tried to get him to tell me what was wrong, but the more I asked, the more certain he became that I was persecuting him. And then came the prelims. He was caught cheating by the monitor, and it was out of my hands. Sin-Jun had no choice but to send him down.'

Davina leaned her head back against the headrest of the chair. 'So he was . . . ill,' she said flatly. She didn't, for one instant, suspect that Gareth was lying to her.

'There's more,' Gareth warned.

'It's going to hurt, isn't it?' she said softly.

Gareth looked up at her and nodded. 'Yes,' he said softly. 'I'm afraid it is.'

'Tell me.'

He took a deep breath. 'At the inquest, the coroner concluded that he couldn't have known about the tumour. His GP testified that he'd never come to him about it.'

Davina frowned. 'So . . . ?'

Gareth glanced once more at the paper. Then, wordlessly, he handed the letter over. As he did so, he knew that he was taking a chance. He was handing her fresh ammunition that she could use against him. Withholding information from a coroner was enough to ruin him every bit as effectively as the exam-papers-for-money scandal she'd thought up. But he knew she would never use it against him. Not now. Now he would trust her with his life. Why not? He already trusted her with his heart, his body, his soul. Davina took the paper, instantly recognising her brother's handwriting.

She took a deep, ragged breath, and began to read.

Dear Dr Lacey,

I thought I'd write this letter to you while I still can. I don't really know how to begin though. Last Michaelmas Term I started having headaches, but then they seemed to go away. Or rather . . . I think, now, that I just forgot that I'd had them. I began to lose time, you see. I'd start to write an essay, and then suddenly find I'd written four pages, but not remember a word until I read my own handwriting to see what I'd put down.

So I went up north, to a private clinic. Of course, they found something nasty on the old brain. But then I knew they would. They tried to be kind, I know. Talked about my 'options', if they could really be considered that. What it amounted to was the fact that I was going to die, stark raving mad, in some hospital somewhere. And I thought . . . well, bugger that!

So I bought the aspirins. Anyway, there's something I meant to tell you. I know I've done something weird. Told someone, I think, that what happened to me was all your fault. I remember writing. But I can't think to whom. I don't want you to feel guilty.

Oh, one other thing. Please don't tell anyone that I know about the tumour. I don't want Mum knowing that I knew. It'd break her heart.

I think that's the lot. I always liked you — I don't know whether I ever told you that. Anyway.

All the best, David.

Davina slowly lowered the rambling letter to the table-top. Tears flooded her eyes. 'Oh, David,' she gulped.

She cried bitterly then, for a long, long time. Gareth watched her helplessly, tears in his own eyes. Finally, when she'd stopped, he silently handed her his handkerchief, then picked up the letter and put it back in the folder.

'You could sense him struggling to keep his mind on what he was doing,' Davina said at last, her voice so faint it was almost a whisper. She closed her eyes briefly. Oh, David!

But it wasn't his fault. None of this was his fault.

Slowly she opened her eyes again. 'David's gone now,' she said simply. 'Now I know the truth. I've just said good-bye to him. Now, this minute. I should have said goodbye at his funeral, but I didn't. I couldn't. Not while I thought he was there because of you.' Her voice was sweet again. Simple. Honest.

Gareth turned and looked at her. 'I know,' he said sim-ply. 'Believe me. I understand.'

Davina took a deep breath. She got up, her legs feeling as weak as water. She walked towards him, one hand held out uncertainly, and he watched her, his eyes shuttered. He had no idea what she was going to do next. Only knew that, whatever it was, it would decide their destiny.

'Gareth,' she said forlornly. 'I'm so sorry. About Gavin Brock. About not trusting you. I should have listened to my instincts, but I didn't.'

Gareth shook his head. What did it matter? What was past was over and done with. It was the future that mattered.

'Oh, Gareth,' she said sadly. 'What are we going to do now?'

Gareth looked at her bleakly. 'Why ask me?' he laughed. 'I don't know. It's up to you.'

'Do you hate me?' Davina asked.

'No.'

'You should. You have the right.'

'Fine,' he said wearily. 'So I have the right to hate you. I'll bear that in mind for the future.'

Davina's cat-green eyes flashed. 'Future? What future? You don't really think we have a future, do you?'

And suddenly, with that returning flash of spirit, he felt his heart leap. He laughed. He couldn't help it. Davina was back! Everything was going to be all right. He couldn't have said why, exactly, he was so certain. He only knew that he was.

'Why not?' he demanded. 'The future's ours to do what we like with. It always has been.' And suddenly he reached for her. Davina had time only to give a quick, surprised squeak, and then she was in his arms. His head swooped, and their lips met in a kiss that rocked them both. His tongue pushed her lips apart, invading her, demanding and receiving the honeyed sweetness of her mouth.

His arms locked into a vice. For the first time since he'd met her, she was his. All his. And he was never going to let her go. When he lifted his head, his eyes were dancing. 'I've been waiting to do that for a long time.'

'Do what?' she gasped, bewildered.

'Kiss you.'

'You've kissed me before.'

'Not like that.'

And Davina suddenly understood what he meant. The truth that surpassed all other truths. That was their first kiss as equals. Not as hunter and hunted. But as real, true lovers.

'Do you mean . . .' she breathed, hardly daring to hope. 'Do you mean you want us to try again?'

'Yes,' Gareth said, no doubt whatsoever in his voice. Others might think he was mad, but what did they matter to Davina and him? They were Moth and Flame. A whole world in themselves. They lived by their own rules. 'Davina, I love you,' he said simply.

'But . . .'

'Do you love me?' he demanded quietly.

'Yes. Oh yes!'

'Do you believe that I love you?'

'Yes.'

'Well, there you are then.'

It was hardly poetical. But they were the sweetest words Davina had ever heard.

TWENTY

Jared rose and stretched, feeling relaxed and happy. His body seemed to glow with the remembrance of their love-making, and as he pulled on his shirt and jeans, he was smiling. He'd have to take her home to meet his mum and dad.

He'd have to buy a ring! Right now he didn't even have any idea what sort of stone she'd like. He'd have to ask her. Still humming to himself, he left his rooms and casually jogged down the stairs.

* * *

Alicia glanced out of the window and sighed. It was not a sad sigh but one of utter contentment. Her life was her own, at last. Hers and Jared's. She too contemplated her family's reaction to her engagement. She doubted it would be one of joy, but they'd get used to it. They'd have to.

She heard a tap on the door, and, without any presentiment of fear whatsoever, opened it.

* * *

Emily, lying on her bed in the room next door, turned the page of the medical textbook she was reading and groaned out loud. Bowel parasites. Charming!

* * *

Alicia bit back a small cry of nervous surprise as Rupert smiled down at her. 'Hello, darling. Can I come in?' And he pushed past her before she could protest.

'But—' Alicia began, then took a deep breath and rubbed her hands nervously across her thighs. She needed to stay calm, keep her tone easy and light.

She watched him walk slowly into the room, looking around him with open interest. Of course, he'd never been here before, she realised. Rupert hesitated over a poster on one wall — a vivid sunset, with a verse from Shelley at the bottom. 'Beautiful,' he said softly. And fingered the sharp silver knife in his pocket.

Alicia frowned. She wished she didn't feel so helpless. So guilty. Rupert came back towards her, where she was still standing more or less in the middle of the floor. Something about the way he looked scared her. His face had a kind of . . . dreamy, elsewhere expression that instantly had the hackles on her neck rising.

* * *

Jared shivered as a blast of cold wind suddenly buffeted him and glanced up at the sky and hurried across Wallace Quad, towards Webster. And Alicia.

* * *

'So, are you thinking of signing up for any more amateur dramatics?' Alicia asked desperately, aware that her voice was squeaking. She was backing away from him now, heading towards the window, where there would be a desk between them.

All right, so he wasn't saying anything. All right, so he was looking at her as if he wanted to devour her with eyes. All right, so he kept putting his hand in his coat pocket and caressing something in there. That didn't mean . . .

Rupert drew out the knife. It glinted in silvery, icy fire in the waning, stormy light. 'It's time, Alicia,' he said softly. 'Isn't it?'

* * *

Jared pushed open the door to Webster's hall and began to take the steps two at a time. Sapphires perhaps? Hell, he was just a man. What did he know about stones? She might surprise him and say she wanted a . . . bloodstone, or opal, or something.

* * *

Alicia stared at the knife, forcing her brain to believe what her eyes were seeing. But it was so hard.

Things like this couldn't happen . . .

He moved towards her, not fast, not sneaky, but still with that slow, dreamy, almost hypnotised smile on his face.

Alicia shook her head, grappling with the feeling of unreality. Keep him talking, a voice piped up from somewhere in the back of her head.

'What do you mean, Rupert?' her voice came out in a dry croak. She backed away another step, her eyes glued to the knife. This was crazy . . .

* * *

Jared got to the top of the stairs and began to whistle slowly under his breath. It was the 'Wedding March'.

* * *

'Rupert,' Alicia tried again. 'What do you want that knife for?'

'Knife?' Rupert asked vaguely. He glanced at the knife in his hand, then back to her. His eyes wore a puzzled frown. 'Well, it's for you, silly,' he said, his voice light and teasing now. 'Just like you wanted.'

Alicia shook her head. 'I don't want a knife, Rupert. I think you'd better take it back to the butler.'

Rupert hesitated, surprised. 'You don't want it?' He frowned. Had he got it wrong? No, she was just nervous now that he was here at last. It was only to be expected.

He smiled. 'It'll be really sweet, Alicia, I promise,' he said softly. 'Do you want me to kill myself too, afterwards, or do you want me to live and suffer?'

Alicia blinked. He's gone, she thought bleakly. Oh, Rupert! Her heart ached, for a single moment overriding her fear, drowning out every other emotion in a wave of tender pity. Oh, Rupert! I'm so sorry. Her eyes filled with tears. She shook her head.

Rupert cocked his head to one side, puzzled. Then realised — she was leaving it up to him what he did afterwards. He nodded and raised his hand. The knife blade caught a gleam of dull light from the window, and it glinted, glacier-like, in the darkening room.

Alicia wasn't even aware of thinking. Barely felt herself move, even. But, the next instant, the chair was in her hands. And she was turning, lifting it up in front of her. Rupert was surprised by her sudden movement, hideously aware that something was not right. She shouldn't be doing this. This is not how their final scene was supposed to be at all. But he was already lunging forward, too late to stop the impetus of the knife strike.

It struck the seat of the chair with a sharp 'twang' of sound. It seemed to free her from her state of denial, and at last Alicia opened her mouth and screamed.

She screamed loudly, desperately, and with everything in her.

In the room next door, Emily fell off her bed. She scrambled to her feet, her heart racing, and yanked open her door. 'Alicia!' she yelled desperately.

* * *

Jared had been halfway down the corridor when he heard Alicia scream and burst into a frantic run. His heart in his throat, a prayer in his heart, and his body bathed in animal fear, he got to Alicia's door and thrust it open.

* * *

Rupert had retracted the knife from the wood by this time and grabbed the leg of the chair being brandished in his face.

'Alicia, stop it!' he admonished, and at that moment, the door behind them burst open. Jared and Emily both tumbled in, then stopped dead in the centre of the room. Emily took in the situation with a horrified glance, her freckles standing out starkly in her ash-pale face.

Jared was much more aware of Alicia first — she was alive! Then he took in the chair she was holding up in front of her, the way she was shaking, the look of terror in her eyes. When Rupert turned, utterly surprised at the intrusion, Jared saw the knife. And he became strangely calm. He realised there were far too many people in the room, and he reached behind him and gestured Emily to leave.

She backed out, then raced down the corridor. She was running before she even knew where she was going, but when she flew down the stairs and into the hall, she turned automatically towards the admin offices, which were, luckily for them all, situated in Webster. In extremis, all St Bede's students turned inevitably to one person: Sin-Jun.

* * *

'What are you doing here?' Rupert asked Jared, his voice curiously pettish. 'You're not supposed to be here.'

Jared glanced questioningly at Alicia, who looked blankly back at him. He saw her begin to sway.

'Unless,' Rupert said, suddenly seeing the light, 'I'm supposed to kill you too. Is that right, Alicia?' he began to turn back towards her.

Jared, desperate to keep him away from Alicia, to keep him from even thinking about her, said quickly, loudly, 'Yes, that's right. You have to kill me first.'

'Jared, no!' Alicia gasped. But it was too late. With a snarl, Rupert launched himself on Jared. He didn't have to make it beautiful for him!

* * *

Sin-Jun looked up, astonished, as a ginger-haired virago erupted into his office, his secretary ineffectively trotting in behind her, an outraged look on her face. 'You've got to come . . .' Emily panted. 'To . . . to Alicia's room. Rupert's got a knife!'

He surged to his feet. 'Where are they?' he barked.

Emily gulped. 'Webster. Room twenty-eight.' Before she'd even finished speaking, Sin-Jun was out of the room. For an old man, he moved very, very fast.

* * *

Jared grunted as he felt himself being slammed back against the wall. His hand came out instinctively to grip Rupert's wrist and the knife missed his face by inches. Rupert was incredibly, ferociously strong. In fact, he had a madman's strength. Jared knew, in that instant, that he was never going to be able to fight him off. He knew a single second of stark fear, then a certain, calming acceptance. All right. He was going to die. If only he could do enough damage first to stop the madman from killing Alicia too.

194

Emily must have gone for help . . . If he could just keep Rupert distracted for a few more minutes . . .

With a snarl Rupert drew his hand free and got ready for another lunge.

Desperately, Jared reached again for his arm. Too late.

Alicia gave another scream, this time carrying clearly to the principal, who was already on the stairs.

Knowing that Jared was only moments away from being stabbed to death, Alicia tossed the chair aside, and, without a single second's hesitation, launched herself at Rupert. She leapt on to his back like a wildcat, clawing his face, screaming something — she didn't know what — over and over again. Rupert gave a shout of surprise and Jared shuddered as the knife scraped by the wall just an inch from his cheek.

Sin-Jun erupted into the room and took in the scene in one glance. The girl on Lord Rupert's back, the boy, Jared Cowan, pinned to the wall, desperately holding on to Rupert's wrist, the glint of the knife. Sin-Jun strode across the room, peeled Alicia off as if she were a piece of rice paper, and aimed a single, clever blow to the back of Rupert's neck. Sin-Jun hadn't been in the army for over twenty years without learning a trick or two.

Without a sound, the Lord of the Realm crumpled to the floor with barely a sigh, utterly unconscious.

Jared staggered from the wall and towards Alicia, who was still lying on the bed where the principal had tossed her. She lifted up her arms mutely and he held her close.

After that there was an ambulance to call, the Earl of Warrington to inform, and any other number of unpleasant but necessary duties. Alicia and Jared simply sat on the bed together, Jared holding her so tightly she could hardly breathe, rocking her to and fro, stroking her hair, and thanking God he hadn't lost her.

Finally, Alicia slowly looked up at him, and managed a small, tremulous smile. 'I was so happy to see you come in that door,' she said, which had to be the understatement of

195

her life. 'But why did you come? I thought when I left we'd agreed to meet up in Hall.'

Jared smiled. 'Oh. That. I wanted to ask you what stone you wanted for your engagement ring.'

Alicia laughed. 'An emerald of course. What else?'

Jared began to laugh too. 'What else?'

He kissed her, oblivious to Emily, oblivious to the principal, oblivious even to the unconscious man on the floor. He had his Alicia. And would have her for the rest of his life. That was all that mattered in the world . . .

* * *

'So, what do you think?' Gareth Lacey said, standing outside the cottage in Duns Tew. It bore a freshly carved wooden nameplate, 'Spindlewood Cottage', which swung in the April wind.

'It's home,' Davina said simply. She tucked her arm inside his, looking at the thatched cottage with a sense of ownership and pride she'd never felt for any other building in her life.

Gareth knew how much that simple statement meant.

He looked down at her spiky blonde head and, with a gentle finger under her chin, tipped her face up to his. 'But it's not a prison,' he said, his storm-grey eyes looking deeply into hers. 'Whenever you want to go off to Bora Bora, or gold mining in Alaska, or whatever, just go. We'll be here waiting for you when you get back.'

'I know,' Davina said, her eyes glowing. 'I know you will.' Never had a man understood her so thoroughly.

'Well, shall I carry you over the threshold?' Gareth asked, turning to her, reaching down to cup his arms under her legs. 'Since it's probably the only chance I'll get . . . ?' he looked up at her questioningly.

Davina laughed. It was the most roundabout way of proposing she'd ever heard. But she didn't take him up on it. Marriage was something that had always frightened her.

Perhaps in ten years' time?

She raised one eyebrow. 'Why does it always have to be the man to carry the woman across the threshold?' she asked. 'I could carry you across instead.' She suddenly ducked, reaching for his own legs.

'Hey! Not fair!' he yelped, ducking again, grabbing her legs and hoisting her over his shoulder in a fireman's lift.

'This is not carrying me over the threshold!' Davina yelped indignantly as he walked up the garden path and opened the door. But it would do.

Oh yes, Davina thought, her heart racing.

It would most definitely do.

THE END

ALSO BY MAXINE BARRY

THE LYING GAME
AN OXFORD REVENGE
More coming soon!

Don't miss the next Maxine Barry release,
join our mailing list:

www.joffebooks.com

ALSO BY FAITH MARTIN

MONICA NOBLE MYSTERIES

JENNY STARLING MYSTERIES

**Join our mailing list to be the first to
hear about NEW FAITH MARTIN releases!**
www.joffebooks.com/contact/

FREE KINDLE BOOKS AND OFFERS

Do you love mysteries, historical fiction and romance? Join 1000s of readers enjoying great books through our mailing list. You'll get new releases and great deals every week from one of the UK's leading independent publishers.

Join today, and you'll get your first bargain book this month!

Follow us on Facebook, Twitter and Instagram @joffebooks

DO YOU LOVE FREE AND BARGAIN BOOKS?

We hate typos too but sometimes they slip through. Please send any errors you find to corrections@joffebooks. com. We'll get them fixed ASAP. We're very grateful to eagle-eyed readers who take the time to contact us.